Woman in the Window

Tales of Desire, Passion and Love

Edited By

PAMELA PRATT

With Special Artwork By

NINA SILVER

STARbooks Press
Sarasota, Florida

─────────────── ♀ ───────────────

Library of Congress Card Catalogue No. 91-068409
ISBN 1-877978-32-9

This book has been printed in the United States of America, and
funded in part by a grant from The Florida Literary Foundation.

For a complete catalogue of selected books, gifts, and other
collectibles available from STARbooks Press and The Florida Literary
Foundation, write: P. O. Box 2737, Sarasota, FL 34230-2737.

Concept and Production Design: P. J. Powers
Cover Art: D. King, Ringling School of Art, Sarasota, FL
Typesetting: A. M. Daspit

CONTENTS

Introduction

INTRODUCTION

I.

The stories in this anthology of lesbian short fiction examine our sexualities, sensibilities, and our many places in the world. The stories are erotic, in all the many ways that it is possible and necessary. Attraction, in all its elements, is explored – from the emotional to the political to states of desire and fulfillment. The stories examine women who are coming together for the first time or continuing ongoing relationships, as well as the place in our minds and hearts and bodies where our fantasies or the fantastic come true.

Openly and honestly, the authors have put into words where we are in the world: words that mark political, social and sexual climates, but go far past that, to the essence of lesbian sensibility. What is important is how (and we know why) we exist as lesbians – that which motivates and moves us, what it means to *be lesbian*. I could use the word "priorities", but to me it goes past that, to something so heartfelt that, to survive, there is no other choice worth considering: something so necessary to us that it is close to the will to live. Our sensibilities, politics, and sexualities are the substance, to me, of what our lives are about. What motivated me to edit this anthology is the necessity I feel to record, in a substantial, recognizable, undeniable form, where we have been, where we are in 1993, and where we are going in the world.

In society at large, the lesbian experience is often looked at in only one way: a minor, paltry existence. But hear us, women who live these lives – happily, grandly, sexually, actively, positively – and we will tell you of the richness of the love, joy and desire that rule our lives. These portrayals of lesbians are, even if fictional, certainly representative.

Diversity and change mark our lives: differences made of up race, age, life style, religion, locale, economics and experience. With all these differences, we are still foremost a community held together by a tie that truly binds us, that we are all women loving women. In this collection of short stories, lesbian authors celebrate our differences as well as our commonality.

Although the stories in this book emphasize the strength, political commitment, desire and joy inherent in our lives and our community, the impact of homophobia is apparent in a few of the stories. Our truths are often curtailed, circumscribed, by the outside world. Hate and fear teach us caution: the language we know best, the language of freedom, many of us have to deny. The understanding of the caution so many of us have to use with the world can begin so early, even before we have seen for ourselves the difficulties that complete honesty can bring, as in Nina Silver's *The Maturing Of Mooghan*, where the character knows instinctively, and at a very young age, what not to say aloud to her parent. Lesléa Newman's character in *Monday Night At The Movies*, makes a stand against homophobia. In *The Repercussions Of Love*, my character finds a spiritual way to fight.

There is another kind of circumspection – one felt by humankind in general – that of people who like each other but may not know each other well. The hesitancy that occurs when a relationship is undefined, and may or may not come to pass, as in the title story by Patricia Roth Schwartz, *The Woman In The Window*, in *Carrot Juice*, by Donna Allegra, *The Ad*, by Tori Joseph, and Maureen Brady's *Care In The Holding*, among others. In other of the stories, lesbians just go ahead and get on with their lives, letting others find a way to work it out, as in Deborah Kay Ferrell's *In Front Of Everybody*, and Dianna Hunter's *Among The Creatures Of Habit*. Because the import of the action/dialogue in the majority of the stories occurs in a lesbian environment, we are given a feeling of warmth, comfort, and recognition.

II.

I regret that I don't know all the authors personally, but those whom I do know I would like to comment about; some things not mentioned in their "official" biographies which appear at the end of the book. Their personal and work-a-day lives resonate with who they are and their convictions, and show an honest way of living as who we are, less encumbered by the prejudices of our families, jobs, locales.

Donna Allegra lives her life in the realms of dance and writing. Her main concerns are racism and homophobia. She lives her life (as much as possible, meaning excluding the work-a-day world) as a Black lesbian. Donna is a construction worker. When she needs to escape the prejudices of her work environment, she leaves the worksite and retires to the Port-o-San to write.

Sarah Schulman, writer of *Prologue*, is the author of several lesbian novels, and is very active in the lesbian and gay community. I first met her several years ago, when interviewing her for a gay New York newspaper. Her third novel, the first for a mainstream publisher, had just come out, and her (continued) success at this – that she makes a living out of the necessity of defining and exploring of our lives – has always given me confidence that what we, as artists, want to do, can be accomplished.

Lesléa Newman, a Jewish lesbian, has thirteen books out to date, and has been able to make her living through her books and teaching "Writing From The Heart", a series of writing workshops for women.

Patricia Roth Schwartz has fulfilled her desire to own the farm in central New York which she dreamed of during all her years in the Boston area. She raises organic produce and Christmas trees. Although she lives in a closeted area, she has established a supportive network of lesbians and gay males. Patricia is in the process of turning a large portion of her farm into a community project for the low income of the area. When I last visited her there, I dreamed intensely and detail of a writers' conference on her land, and she now has plans to have her first women writers' weekend there this coming summer.

Karen Moulding, a lawyer, has not been in New York long, but immediately threw herself into the community head first. She uses her law skills in the fight against AIDS by being very involved with ACT-UP – and where better could we employ a lawyer?

I have, since my teenage years, never taken a job where I couldn't be positively acknowledged for who I am. I work among artists and political activists who, although some are not homosexual themselves, are supportive and at ease with gayness. As the years progress, I have made (economically unsound) choices that have allowed me the freedom to exist in the sexual, social, and political community necessary to me.

I mention these details because, to me, our lives are as positive and affirming as our stories are. We live exciting and useful lives, as moving and enlightening as the lesbians we have written about. We all have disappointments – illness, lovers leaving us or us having to leave them, the economy – no one can completely escape these things – but in these pages what you will hear is confirmation of the joy and strength of lesbian lives. I give you a book of truth.

PROUD YONI

SHOES

Claire Olivia Moed

I got a friend, Settagrea. She got 42 pairs of shoes. All black. The heels start very demurely and then rise in height depending on how much she wants to fuck you. She's my ex. We never got past two inch heels. I wasn't ready for it. And she wanted more. So one night I tried to please her, but got too high. Broke my ankle. Broke her heart. That was years ago.

One night, last night, in the heat of my want, but no relief in sight I go to Settagrea's house. I'm different this time. I ain't afraid of heights. I come up to the steps of her walk-up. I call her.

"Settagrea, you got the shoes. I want 'em."

She buzzes me in.

The apartment is her closet. She never has to leave. Like living in Macy's all the time. Something to always try on. How could you possibly get bored? I know after I left her for a pair of sneakers and a paint brush - Selma - Settagrea, she took out all her black dresses and the few red ones, and all her black jeans and bras and nightgowns and hats and set up her wardrobe from one end of the apartment to the other. No books.

It is the last wall, with the windows facing the street noise, that's where the garter belts and the 42 pairs of shoes live. 42 pairs of shoes in a double door china closet – double doors, missing all the glass. 42 pairs.

I go straight to the window. The other rooms are a thing of the past and I don't got time for memories tonight.

Settagrea lights a cigarette. She exhales and tongues me deep like it's a joint she's been toking and she wants to shotgun me some homegrown organic weed. But Settagrea, she knows I'm trying on sober so she keeps it to Marlboros and Merits. I suck it up.

She's wearing not much and it's tight. Her heels are three-inch patent spikes. She's thinking of going out and taking a walk. Outside it's dark, and the lights in the dark crack and pop like multi-orgasms about to happen. Settagrea's in heat. She takes a look at me, I might as well be coming in front of her that's how well she knows me. And she knows I'm in heat too and we're nearly useless to each other but we're gonna try and rectify that anyway.

"Settagrea, I wanna go higher than before. Some serious high heel, a black garter belt, the skirt you're wearing and a tight bra I don't own. It's the only way I'm gonna get through the night not fucking a stranger who wants to eat my soul for breakfast."

Settagrea, she nods. Takes a pair from the no glass china door, rubs the dust off them across her breasts. I've always liked Settagrea's breasts. They're so damn demanding.

These shoe's she's got, they're black and tall and very mean and shiny. They're a half-inch taller than the rest.

Settagrea says, "I fucked a millionaire in these, then sent her home in a taxi I paid for. They're very powerful shoes. If Dorothy had clicked them, she would of ended up in France."

My breathing is faster than I am. "They're nice."

She tells me, "Take off your pants. All of them." She pulls out of somewhere a pair of black seamed stockings with pink edges and an extra garter belt. It's black too, got silver snakes as the clamps. I pull off my jeans so fast they go inside out. My panties are now officially missing. Except for my tee shirt, I'm buck naked.

Settagrea pushes me into the arm chair facing the windows. She grabs a small stool, straddles it, and takes my leg and begins to slowly roll the stocking up my calf.

The two gay guys from across the street come to their window. They nod and sit down to watch. Ever since their TV got stolen, Settagrea has been their personal PBS station. They appreciate good art.

She's rolling past my knee. I groan inside. I give in. Everything. Desire as a cess pool I'm imprisoned in. I remember in that movie, "Seven Beauties", the man who drowns himself in the shit pit because it was a better option than living in Nazi chains. One hell for another. I give in.

Settagrea dangles the garter in front of me. The snake clamps are dancing and swiggling and undulating. Settagrea does not smile. She just looks at me. Me? I look at the snakes.

Finally, an order. "Pull it over your head."

She throws it at me and I shimmy it down my breasts, my stomach and get it comfortable around my ass and hips. The gay boys applaud. They like realism.

She does not offer the cigarette. It is understood that I'd better take it to complete the outfit. The outfit is what counts here. I take it, she lights it, I suck it, oh baby, I'm gone.

She starts rolling nylon up the other leg. The gay boys are kissing. They feel bonded to us, and us to them. That's why we let 'em watch. It's family.

All my snakes are now chomping and dancing on my stockings.

Settagrea holds the heels up. I watch them cause they're living, breathing dragons of fire and fuck me grunts. I'm going to be wearing live dragons on my feet. I can't even speak at this point.

She puts my right foot in between her breasts. Dragons don't like cold toes. She blows into the right shoe, just to make it happy and then slips it on. My leg comes alive. I am alive. Power that paid for a rich girl's cab shoots straight up into my crotch. I start to sweat.

Settagrea snaps her fingers for the other foot. The sound hasn't left her hand and my left foot is smack right into her cleavage. She lifts a toe into her mouth, nips it gently, runs her tongue around the heel and then licks so fucking slow the arch of my foot. Her tongue draws a line between point A and point B, but it's taking the scenic route.

She rolls and rubs her head into my heel. There is a silence before a moan. Then she takes the other shoe and slips it on. Cinderella shoulda been a dyke. Maybe she was. A woman willing to trade her whole life just because the shoe fit.

Settagrea strokes my leg up to the dancing, eating snakes and says, "The right to wear my skirt left the day you did. But you look good as it is. So sit back and smoke baby. Just smoke."

She stands up, and gives me a deep kiss from lips other than the ones on her face, goes to the door, and says, "I'm going for a walk." Then she's gone. I lick up her kiss, smoke a smoke and I laugh and laugh and laugh and laugh and I watch the life I live from Settagrea's window.

Part 8 from "Driven By Passion, Run Over By Love" a book/performance piece (and birthday present) to J. L. Wong.

CARROT JUICE

Donna Allegra

I was getting ready for the kill as soon as the light changed or the traffic let up at 20th Street, going uptown along Park Avenue South when I glimpsed this battered green Peugeot passing my brand-new silver Atala. I was slightly miffed but when I saw it carried a sister, I adjusted my attitude and decided to check her out. I caught up at 23rd Street where she stood half-woman, half-metal, fluid focus, oblivious to the rush-hour traffic and my hard cruise.

She just straight out-of-the-blue rolled her bike back and asked, "You in a hurry?" with no introduction or apology. I was so pleased at this cute little babe talking to me like we'd been long-time buddies, that I didn't miss a beat either. I shrugged, "No hurry."

I was game and I'm no slouch. I was out on the bike just to take a cruise around my estate, so I had plenty time. I followed her lead and we crossed the avenue during the red and then cut over the street on the green. She rides good, just like me, tagging the tail of a bus through a changing light and begging mercy off the car she cut off at the next corner.

That first day she took me up Sixth Avenue into Central Park to a place where the rows of trees and rows of statues stood still and noble and said, "Isn't this lovely?" It was just at sunset; the sun had finished dozing purple and was off to dreaming pink and orange and the trees were half-dressed in spring growth. It was grand and I said yes and she said, "I needed to show it off to someone."

I decided right then and there: I like this girl, and it was odd that I was inclined towards her. The only thing we had in common was two-wheel drive. She's one of those righteous roots-and-herbs sisters with a Muslim name, Pan-African hippie style who greets you with "Peace" and says 'bye with "Love."

She looked at me with clear dark eyes like she was reading into my head, put her hand to my heart and said "See you" like indeed we were friends for life who would hook up later. She was gone when I realized with regret I probably would not see her for a long time to come, and it would be by accident at that.

Maybe three weeks later, I was out taking another tour of my estate, this time by Union Square Park, which was temporarily transformed by the flowers, fruit and vegetable sellers getting more business than the loose jays and coke crowd. I'd gotten some of that good Chock full 'o nuts coffee - or maybe it was the creamer that I liked so much - and was looking for a space to cool out with the trees and away from the dealers so I could watch the Farmers Market show when who should I see a few benches down, but the green Peugeot and Khalilah - that's her made-up real name. She was munching away on some raw red peppers and green pea pods. I might've could've dealt with the red peppers, but she was chomping away on the green pea pods and looked just as pleased as a body could be. I couldn't hack it myself. It seemed bad enough to have to eat the shit plain, but raw?

I looked into my bag for some domino sugar packets to offer the child, then thought better of it and decided on the sweet 'n low. It wasn't sugar, it was a naturally man-made scientific chemical, so to me that meant organic. After all, scientists could do it better than Nature could ever plan it.

That's when I started calling her "Carrot Juice." She shined with laughter at my offer, the red highlighting her caramel skin. She's a crunchy granola kid who looks like Health, Nutrition and Moderation in Everything, whereas I'm a 100% beef and cholesterol carnivore freak. Candy bars and make-up are perfectly natural to me.

Now I know what you're thinking, but Carrot Juice was just not my type. I like my women at least as butch as I am, and I don't tell that to everyone because some people will act like they just do not understand or they won't take how it means to me. The newly-born feminists especially get all riled. They claim that there's no such animal: butch amd femme don't exist;

butch is male-identified, femininity is a social construct and so on, you know the rap. With another butch, I feel safer to be straight-up for real. I don't have to worry about minding my manners to impress her.

No, Carrot Juice/Khalilah wasn't my kind of girl, but she was definitely intriguing. Since it seemed like the universe had it in for us to hook up, I set my coffee and packets of sweetener on the bench. After I locked my front wheel to the frame and lay the bike on her side where I could keep an eye and a foot on her, Khalilah said, "You have a patch kit on you? I've got a broken leg," pointing to her front wheel flat, then adding "And I'm not good on my feet."

I knew what she meant. I hated walking. If I have to go to the store around the corner, I'll take the bike. If I'm invited somewhere that the bike can't come inside for her safety, I don't go. My trusty steed serves me well and it's second-nature to protect her.

Khalilah hooked my tire irons to her spokes and under the tire, then peeled around the rim, like she was taking the skin off an apple. She handed me the inner tube while she checked inside the tire for the offending piece of glass. I pumped the tube up, heard the telltale hiss and patched the hole.

Five minutes later she had two wheels to ride on. She smiled like a proud parent and patted her seat saying, "You were a good girl while Mommy and the doctor fixed you." Her chain clicked into gear like a cat purring.

We split up again without exchanging phone numbers and all day Sunday I cursed myself for being such a cool fool and not asking for hers.

. . .

On Monday I went back to work. I'm in construction. That's what I tell folks and the girls go ooh and ahh, but technically, I'm a waitress at a coffee shop across the street from a construction site at City College. Every day I have to walk under the scaffolding where the door to the construction worker's entrance has drawings of women's bodies emphasizing the breasts and targeting the vagina. Men's cocks were pictured all over the wall.

Construction guys are really raunchy about their dicks. I'd be bringing eggs, sausage, toast and coffee to a table and hear some guy bragging about "...all that good hot pussy I got this morning." I don't believe a word of it when these dudes talk about who they fuck and how much they're getting. Half of them are impotent and the other half are closet queens scared to come out, because of what their friends might say. And after all the alcohol they consume, they can't get anything up. I don't think they fuck anyone without paying for it. Who'd want to sleep with them? Women aren't stupid.

. . .

The counter for morning coffee is a traffic jam with everyone hustling to get a position on the highway out to breakfast. The two Georges and me are the road the customers ride. We navigate our orders, driving teas with milk, wheat toast, fried eggs on rolls, juice, two scrambled, double with bacon salt pepper ketchup.

The morning Khalilah walked in with a tool bag on the side of her hip, I nearly dropped a double egg with bacon and cheese and a buttered blueberry muffin right in a sheet metal worker's lap. He belly-ached about getting his food shaken up like that, but he wasn't about to send it back.

Khalilah was an apprentice electrician and had been transferred up here where the endless City College reconstruction work was going on. She was doing the morning coffee run for her crew and it just seemed like fate that now I'd be seeing her daily.

. . .

By Friday my newfound friend was glum behind the men in her gang jerking her around, unaware that girls don't like being told what to do as if they are stupid. Instead of the four teas with milk, five coffees light, two teas with lemon, three Sankas, two hot chocolates; two buttered bagels, one bialy light on butter, one buttered roll, one toast with cream cheese; two double eggs with cheese, two toasted blue, one toasted corn and two english she'd written up as the order, she asked for sixteen black coffees and told me to lay them out first so they'd get cold and fourteen of the funkier plain rolls, no sugar. She also asked George II for some black spray paint.

When she came back for the afternoon coffee run, she wore a big-time smile. She said she'd pay for Sunday dinner - I took that as my formal invitation - with the tip she'd gotten from the morning. She placed the spray paint on the counter and said, "But I told the girl what you guys ordered." She sucked her teeth in disgust about the men in her crew.

"So now I get to hang a couple of those simple-ass lights and not just watch those fuck-offs botch it up, then spend more energy bullshitting the foreman about why they couldn't get the work out than it would have taken them to just do it. Ugh. Men don't work," Khalilah said. "When a job has to be done, they go on over-time, fuck around at half-speed and then get time-and-a-half for it."

When I left for the day, I glanced over by the door to the construction worker's entrance under the scaffolding because something caught my eye. Or rather, something didn't register as it usually did. The drawings of the women's bodies and men's penises weren't there. What I saw were black splotches spray-painted over the door I'd typically frown upon.

Girlfriend could keep a secret. For once I couldn't wait for Saturday to hurry up and get done. I was eager for our dinner date, even it was going to be sea weed, brambles and chlorophyll.

. . .

Around 7:30 I arrived at her block. I rode across E. 10th Street and saw the moon hung low - her lower hips at the other side of Tompkins Square Park. She must have been high, coming down to the East Village like that and looking so luscious naked in the heart of Alphabet City.

I phoned first, to be sure I had the address right. She answered on the third ring, saying, "Peace and love."

"Peas and rice to you too." I said.

She laughed. "Hey girl. How you be?" A lot of folks would put a chill with their righteous attitude against my heathen one. I've said a lot of uncool things to her that she never held against me.

She would live in a 5-flight walk-up. Every dyke in N.Y.C. does. I can understand that you can't be a real lesbian without being owned by a cat and accompanied by a motorcycle escort, but why must a 5-flight walk-up be mandatory for our socio-economic profile?

I put the bike's frame on my shoulder and grumbled my way up the stairs, but I let the peevishness evaporate when I saw Khalilah. She's a downright pretty woman. That affects me somehow. I'm sorta cute, at least at some angles, but there is something about feminine, lovely women that makes me want to slow down and be very careful about getting too close. I'm sure to be the one who gets hooked while she isn't liking me back.

Khalilah's apartment was East Village standard - a three-room railroad, bath tub in the kitchen, a closet-sized space for a pull-chain toilet. At least the jane was inside the place and not down the hall. She might have paid the rent, but the stacks of albums, 45s and cassettes were the real owners of the space; all the piles were snugged neatly along the wall.

Each window held a little mobile or set of chimes hanging in it. When the wind blew from the south into her apartment, the tinkling of the chimes seemed coordinated with the dance of the mobile. The white walls glowed with a blue cast to them, the white curtains were sewn with blue trim.

Her mattress lay on the floor along with one long, and two smaller cushions to sit on. The wood was varnished so lightly that her sanded floor looked inviting. I warmed up to the idea of sitting on the cushions.

The kitchen housed a clean white stove and refrigerator. Its wooden shelves were varnished like the floor. Over the table lay a cloth of African fabric with red geese swooping across an orange sky. The clear glass bowl held ears of corn. One of the ceramic bowls contained pea pods and red peppers that glistened with oil, so I figured they were cooked, thank God. The little white squares mixed in were polka-dotted brown. The other ceramic bowl held broccoli, cauliflower and red cabbage emitting a scent like buttered popcorn. The large stainless steel bowl nestled salad. I could recognize the iceberg lettuce and spinach, but there were several other green leaves whose acquaintance I'd never made.

She saw my suspicious sniffing around, so I said, "I know your tip from the now-famous coffee run didn't cover all these vittles."

"No, but that was just an excuse to lure you into my lair," she said, stripping the green husk off the corn like she was yanking out a nail with a hammer.

"Besides, we ride all the time. Even when we go to a park to hang out after work, there's always all this stuff going on around us. Why not try just us being together?" she addressed the broccoli, cauliflower and cabbage, and I thought: what a sweet little girl.

Our time together had gotten good to me. On our bikes she was my friend and no one else's. I've always been a jealous cuss, feeling a little stung when my pals would connect with each other apart from me. I enjoyed us together: riding through the West Village; talking on the pier at Morton Street to relax in the early evening; but most of all, our morning rides to work.

We'd alternate meeting at the northwest corner of Washington Square Park with the southwest corner of Stuyvesant Square Park. By 7:00 we'd be leaving 6th Avenue at 59th Street and enter Central Park - the grandmother of all the N.Y.C. parklets.

The ride through Central Park in the morning was one of the the most intimate acts I could do with with someone. Here I rode my hour of two wheels-meditation on balance with no hands. My true self would rise and shine without excuse or coverup. I didn't have to be on-guard like at the job or on good behavior like when I was courting a lover. Here I would speak thoughts aloud, form my own opinions about things and not take anyone else into account or be fair and reasonable. Khalilah heard me in my truest form.

Already I liked her in an important way that touched me where I could be hurt and I didn't take that lightly. It bugged me that she was such a beauty. In my book of rules, that meant danger. But because we met on wheels, I didn't feel a need to put on a show to make her like me. With a 10-speed between my legs I was a woman of wheels and wonder.

She started bringing the dinner food into her living room. "The utensils are in the left cabinet. Choose your weapons and bring me a couple of bowls and the red chopsticks." I did as told and sat in front of her on the sea-green cushion.

She worked those chopsticks like a pro, retrieving slivers of lettuce and excavating buds of broccoli. She ate strongly, like a horse pulling its grass from the ground. I even liked her cooking and I have a career investment in the greasy beefys, but the corn was raw. I started to yelp, but found with surprise, "It's sweet. It tastes like candy!"

She batted her eyes at me. Clearly I'd gone for the bait. "Tee hee hee," she said.

That's when I told her that I called her "Carrot Juice" in my mind. She seemed pleased. "Do you really ever think of me?" Well sure I did, and lots, but I couldn't tell her that. There are limits to how close you get to people.

OK, so I was feeling my Wheaties for her, but I couldn't bring myself to cross the line. Besides, she's a classic beauty of colored womanhood; she'll never want me. She may be a hippie now, but she probably grew up knowing she was fine and that was almost as good as being born with high yellow skin, good hair and light eyes. She could be a stone fox if she wanted to, like one of those snooty Essence model types. She probably went for the refined butch or else another well-mannered pretty femme. I couldn't take the chance on being looked over and politely turned away.

She cleared the food and bowls away and we kicked back against the large cushion to listen to music. Her apartment has a great view overlooking Tompkins Square Park with plenty of sky on display. The Isley Brothers' "Make Me Say It Again, Girl" was playing on her record player. The world had darkened outside. The moon was a yellow plate on a dark blue table cloth with salt sprinkles, the stars.

She asked, "Are you...with anyone?"

"No."

She didn't say anything more.

I wondered what that meant coming from her. I was jiggling my feet and my arm pits were moist. I was thinking about what to do when Khalilah took my hand, knitting our fingers, which she studied for a moment, then leaned over and kissed me.

Her mouth was cozy and warm, reminiscent of dinner. I moved over on the cushion so we could get a better fit.

Sometimes I think human beings just aren't designed properly. Bicycles have better engineering for getting between my legs. Not that I had plans for anything naughty, but it felt good to kiss, our tongues slow dancing, my body whimpering for more. I managed to get my arm around her shoulder and pull her closer, to get some butch leverage. She drew away from me for a moment – and oh, the tear to my heart – and shifted so that her back and head lay on the cushion; then pulled me to lie on top of her. I pushed my thigh between her legs and pressed in a rhythm as old as rain. She was the ocean whose waves are a persistent child pleading, "Mommy, listen." Her breath by my ear was the wind chattering through the leaves. I felt like a sunny sky jolted by thunder, all clouds brushed aside.

In my arms I held the waves which earlier had nipped and licked at the shore line, now hurtling themselves up a rocky ledge. They crashed against the cliff to recede into a glistening foam. Her breath that urged the leaves from their branches now whispered secrets.

The lightning had first stroked, then pierced me clear blue to the core. I watched her calmed face, features even, balanced, neat. I wondered what this woman wanted with me. I didn't want to end up left behind when she decided to roll along on her merry way.

I needed time and space to think. When it comes to letting people get this kind of close, I usually go ooh, yuk, cooties. Not that the pretty girls don't turn my head around, but I ride away from really working it out with someone for the long distance.

Khalilah lay very quiet, perhaps even asleep. I kissed her on the cheek and got up. The door locked shut behind me. I took my bike from her hallway and rode home wondering how to hold back the rain.

· · ·

The next morning, we met at the northwest corner of Washington Square Park to ride up to work. Neither of us was talking about it. Khalilah looked to be on the verge of saying something, but not coming up with any words worth a damn.

I acted like nothing happened. "Thanks for dinner. It was nice of you."

"I enjoyed the evening too. I...uh...."

"We better boogie before it gets late. Looks like heavy traffic today."

We rode the rest of the way in silence.

We saw the regulars in Central Park. I'd dubbed one man "the judge," for the high ruddy color in his cheeks. The walk queen's steps outdistanced most joggers, while the anorexic ran in her quick little motions. The bike racers flew past us with a wave and of course, the four-wheel fiends were out in full force.

At 138th Street and Amsterdam Avenue Khalilah had to go into her job site at City College and I had to go into the restaurant. "I'll see you at morning coffee" she called out to me before turning to leave. I avoided her eyes by shouldering the bike, pretending to side-step the bottles smashed in the street from the weekend.

At 9:00 she wasn't there. A new boy with fuzz on his face was trying authoritatively to get my attention at the take-out counter. He gave the order all wrong. "One egg sandwich with bacon and a light coffee, an english muffin with jelly and no butter and a regular coffee. I need a ham sandwich on rye bread with a black tea."

"Hold up, guy. Count up all the coffees, teas and drinks; then the number of bagels, bialys, muffins, toasts and sandwiches for the grill; then give me the numbers. First the food, then the drink order. Here's a box for today, but next time bring your own. What happened to the girl?" That's how construction guys referred to Khalilah.

"I'm the new apprentice, so I'm getting the coffee order for the crew. Oh yeah, I almost forgot. She wants a hot water with lemon. She's got her own tea bag or something."

I felt relieved but pissed. I didn't like this boy. I wanted to see Khalilah, though not to see her. The rest of the day moved like the proverbial slow boat to China.

When I wheeled my bike from the coffee shop, she was waiting for me across the street.

"Hey girl. Wanna go for a ride?"

"Sounds good to me."

At the bottom of Central Park, she said, "How about the pier to talk for a bit?" I nodded. "Let's go down 9th Avenue."

In less than 30 minutes we were at the Morton Street pier. It was like being outside of the city. No rush or crowding took place in the late afternoon. The water of the Hudson River glittered like a rhinestone cape. We walked our bikes past a het couple practicing tai chi and four young Latino queens ragging one another.

"Miss girl. You need to change them clothes. Take it from me and God."

After we set our bikes on their sides she began, "Last night... I wanted to get closer to you and maybe I got side-tracked with the kissing and stuff....I don't always roll over like a bitch in heat after dinner...." She was looking to me for some help with this.

I said, "Hey. It happens. No big thing."

Believe me, I hated myself as the words came out. It was not the cruelest thing I'd ever done. I just wasn't up for being abandoned like a bike locked to a parking meter whose wheels a thief took and the owner decided to junk.

She didn't speak on it, just cringed to herself and said vaguely, "I, uh...gotta go now. I'll...see ya."

I said, "Sure, see ya around...." like I hadn't hurt her to heart and knew it.

I ached into my thighs, regret leaking to the soles of my feet. She'd opened a soft place for me to nestle and I'd shoved her away. I knew I'd done wrong, and now, I didn't want to stay wrong. It's not every day love licks you full in the face.

I saw she'd ridden to West Street and was heading for the West 11th Street exit, not Christopher Street, which would take her clear towards home. I took a guess on where she was heading and mounted my trusty steed. I prayed there'd be no heavy traffic in case she wasn't heading for Madison Square Park because otherwise, I'd lose her, and I might not be so willing to own up to the error of my ways tomorrow.

I was right about her destination of 23rd Street. She'd gone up Sixth Avenue and I'd ridden up Eighth and cut across. It was pure dumb, blessed luck that I saw her on 23rd and Madison. I said, bet, let's head in for the kill, but she didn't go into the park. She kept peddling east.

I followed at a leisurely pace, no longer racing to catch up. She was going to FDR Drive, the park by the water. I watched her from a distance for awhile. I guess it was cowardly of me, but I didn't want to go to her then. I waited until I knew she'd finished crying.

I walked the bike over to her bench, locked it to the railing and sat beside her.

"I'm sorry. I freaked. I was scared you wouldn't want what I wanted as much as I did. Could we try this closeness stuff again?"

She looked at me like she was checking the scale to see if it really was a pound of fruit, like how some people turn over vegetables questioning their quality for cooking.

"Last night wasn't just sex play for me. I turned myself inside out trying to reach you and you disappeared on me. How do I know you won't run away again leaving my belly split open?"

"I can't fix you up with a puncture proof tire on this trip, Khalilah....I dunno."

She said nothing more. Now I had a taste of what it was like to be pulling teeth. I was glad I had the bike with me for protection. She regarded her perfect machine like she was getting ready to mount up and ride off into her own sunset. I was losing faith fast.

I moved closer to her and picked up her hand to try again. "Listen," I said, not knowing what I could say. "Close your eyes."

She frowned, uncertain.

"Let me try to answer you."

She shut her eyes. I cradled her right hand into my left and pressed my right hand's fingers into her palm. The palm is harder to affect, but I stroked it, then the valleys between her fingers. I listened to the air between us as I guided my fingertips down behind the base of her fingers. I mounted my palm against her, circling her mound. My fingers wrapped around the back of her hand, our naked palms hugging. Then I pulled away and slid down. My four fingers and thumb lapped her hand's center.

After a while, I slid up the front wall to caress the length of her down to the core of her hand and up the roots of her fingers to again go over the top. My knuckles went to their knees and circled the belly of her hand. With my thumb I drew curlicues on her wrist. I creeped up once more to hug between her fingers, wrapping the back of her hand into mine. We made a mated pair. I rested my thumb on top of hers; they looked like two heads on a pillow.

"Why don't we try the last few scenes again and you call the shots?" I ventured after a long moment.

Her face held the same expression as when I left her last night.

"So how come I have to direct the action?" she said with a hint of smile.

"Because you're the femme. The femme always wins."

"No, I'm the butch and you're the femme. But you're such a dingo femme you don't know how to act and I have to tell you what to do."

"No," I said. "I'm the butch, you're the femme. You get to have whatever you want from me."

"Oh, is that it? OK. Toasted corn, heavy on the butter, light coffee, extra sugar."

I KISSED HER IN THE STREET

Patricia Roth Schwartz

For us it began this way. We met as usual, in the bar, of course, introduced by mutual friends. What wasn't usual: neither of us bar regulars, neither of us looking. My breakup had been a few months back, hers a lot longer. We were cautious women, cultivating friends, avoiding coupled events. Once scorched, we were now fire-shy.

I liked her. She was handsome: deep eyes, a strong face, a solid body. Solid attracted me: I'd been living with will'o the wisp. She was tall. Tall attracted me: a length like that could shelter a woman. A keen wind, I thought, wouldn't buffet her much. In a bar, with the dimness, the smoke, the jaunty noise of girls who just wanna have fun, undercut with the tonality of two a.m. closing desperation, there was no way to gather in solid, to reach for tall.

We shook hands as our friends bantered on. I wanted to ask for her number. Inside, I was far too raw from the recent ripping out of my heart. Yet as she smiled, said goodbye, murmured the usual, I'll see you again, I felt in, the raw place in my chest, a tiny new bud begin to push up.

Weeks later, at a potluck, my friends breezed in; she was with them, more handsome than ever. In normal light I would see her eyes. I knew they were blue, yet a blue of exceptional darkness, lustre, and depth. Into her, I could lean, yes, and, also, I realized, sink down deep.

Her hips curved under dark corduroy. She was not a wisp. The lines that played at her eyes' corners spoke of maturity, yet in that instant, as she stood near me, not really having a good reason, yet lingering, I yearned to touch the skin of her face, baby-tender.

This time the phone numbers were exchanged, the tentative offers of dinner or lunch or tea suggested. The dance, however haltingly, had begun.

It was Saturday night dinner, then, her place, with our friends as buffer. Candlelight gleamed in those eyes as chicken with lemon and artichokes were served, as the light glanced off the crystal vase in which the flowers I'd brought her rested. Yet her attention was to the guests, to the orderly progression of a social occasion. I felt deflated. I wanted to nuzzle her neck, to touch the soft swell of breasts against the pleated silk shirt, let my hands slide down the velvet length of her slacks, shaping themselves to the curves, to lean into that scented neck, to feel arms encircle me, yes, to lean.

Yet all I could do was pass the salad, offer to pour the wine, ramble on about softball and the latest film, and try to cross my legs hard.

One of our friends had cramps. With a flurry of hugs and well-wishes, we bundled the two out into the night. Suddenly, in her kitchen, by the sink full of dishes, the countertop littered with wine-pooled glasses and serving bowls, we were awkwardly alone. I wanted so much: her touch, her mouth, her laughter against my thigh, the knowledge of her fingers....I settled for a chatty ramble through her video collection, finally settling on nothing. She put on some jazz, we refilled two wine glasses, found the sofa, sat just close enough to be tantalizing, just far enough apart to bespeak sheer terror.

Then, at first haltingly, finally with increasing flow and ease, the talk began. All seemed possible then. I began to know how much I wanted that body, full-length against mine; I wanted to know what kind of cry I could bring from her by my tongue, my touch, the heat of my limbs – yet I wanted, too, the way our thoughts became intertwined, the ease with which I found I could share secrets, dreams, so long locked away, to let loose a little of the pain that had for each of us been a hidden companion.

"I feel so comfortable with you."

She seemed about to reach out – yet everything coiled up and back.

"Me, too."

My own body tightened all over, to hold in what it wanted

to do with hers.

"It's time to get going, though." I was all bustle and energy, then, finding my boots and glasses and car keys.

We were at the door. We were close and I could see how the top of my head – should I just let myself fall against her – would come to her cheekbone, how easily she could kiss my hair. Instead, she kissed my lips. Lightly, so lightly, so quickly I could have missed it. We shared a small hug, the social kind friends always share.

"I'll call you," she said, the kind of things friends always say.

I turned – and it was so hard, that new bud pushing up into the emptiness of my chest, filling me with green growing energy – and opened my car door. As I backed out into the street, I realized that during the evening my rear window had iced over. Keeping the motor running, I jumped out and grabbed for my scraper. She hurried over, having pulled on her ski jacket, concerned.

"It's fine now." I tossed the scraper in the back and turned. With no premediation, only a yearning as old as the earth, I found myself tugging at the fabric of her jacket. I pulled her to me. Our lips met. I kissed her in the street.

Jauntily, I freed her, jumped in the car, and floored it. Ice crystals splintered in my wake. I vanished into the night. Shaking all over, all jauntiness gone, I reached the throughway entrance. My god, I said to myself, breath fogging the car's interior, I can't believe I did that. I kissed her in the street!

Sure I'd driven her away forever, next day I slumped about full of despair and self-loathing. Where was my cool, my self-respect, my intrinsic dyke sensibilities for respecting personal boundaries and space, giving someone permission to go at her own pace, decide for herself where and when she wanted to be more than friends – if indeed, she did? I gagged at my own ineptitude.

The next night she called. "I want to talk about you." Though her tone was cheery, I feared the worst. Be brave, I chanted. Yes, that's fine, I mentally rehearsed. Being friends is good. We've both been hurt. Taking things too quickly is not a good idea. So what if I love your body to distraction, so what if I long to explore all the crevices of your ear with my tongue?

Let us be friends.

"If you're sufficiently over your break-up," she says instead, "I'd like to date you."

"Oh, me, too." I didn't even have to stop to calculate the reply, and so, the next night, after the movies, we found ourselves in her van in the parking lot where we'd left my car, the radio turned low, the heat turned high.

The talk flowed again, even more easily. All topics seemed possible, work, family, past relationships, life itself.

"I have to get going," I said again, checking my watch.

"Oh? So now is it my turn?" Impishly, she reached for my jacket, pulled me to her. As she came closer, I whipped off my glasses. She grinned. I tilted my head so our mouths could meet.

We've been debating it now for a year; usually we laugh together early weekend mornings when we have the time for each other, her place or mine, after we roll ourselves gently from sleep into the languid tender kisses that lead so gradually, with such a sweet heated build-up into a repeat of the fierce roll and tumble of the night before, which of us opened her mouth first, which tongue so boldly, yet gently, sought the other. Yours, she says. No yours, I counter, and we grin.

That kiss, the one that melted my bones and brought a swelling of the bud in my chest that had begun to crack open into flower, has turned into a kind of icon of our loving, a moment I hold now in the palm of my hand.

That week, as our late night confessional phone calls began to reveal, brought little sleep to either of us, as the implications of that erotic exploration began to sink im.

"We need to talk," she said, finally, as the week progressed toward our inevitable Saturday dinner date, again at her place, no other guests.

"We need to talk about what we like, about how we want to make love."

"I think I'm blushing...." I said. "Well...." I touched my hot face. Indeed, I was. "I like everything," I said. "Me, too," she said.

And now, that's the way it is for us, whenever we can clear the space for each other, her place or mine. These days, we favor afternoon movies. We enjoy early candlelight dinners. We put on the music that moves us – and we move.

And I lean. Against that dear and solid and comfortable body that excites me so much, I lean. And she holds me. This way, she says, I hold her, too. Her shoulder cradles my head. Her hand holds my hand agaisnt her heart. Together we sway. We rock. I feel the swell of her breasts, and then she lets both her hands slip down my body to caress me and cradle my bottom with a squeeze. Our center of gravity shifts. As the music gets hotter, we boogie on down. One thigh slips between another thigh. We feel the sweet heat. Our deltas touch and press and begin to throb like hearts. We're kissing by now, of course. We're always kissing. I think we kiss in our dreams, in our thoughts, all day, at work, washing dishes, walking the dogs. Our tongues love each other. Her mouth is the softest place on heaven or earth, I know its fierceness now, too, the questions it asks, the answers it demands.

I'm unbuttoning her silky shirt, my hands curving themselves to the tops of her breasts. She's pulled up my sweater. Her hands find my breasts, smaller, with nipples just as eager. Belt buckles are always next. The first time I pulled down her zipper, I was as jaunty and impish as when I grabbed that jacket. Then I went serious and so did she when my hand slipped down into the space the zipper had freed.

Silky, so silky, I murmer as I caress the hair of her delta, that precious spot above the merging of her thighs, the ones whose silky inner skin I love now to tantalize with my tongue.

Her wetness, her open eagerness that takes me in all the way to the very center, never fails to amaze me each time I encounter it anew. That first time – for, after the dancing, we left a trail of clothing all the way up the stairs to her cool blue-gray loft bedroom under the skylight – she made me wait until much touching and kissing and holding ("I want to hold you – oh, I want so much to hold you!") had happened. And then the gift was given, the gift accepted.

The hard, tight responsiveness of her clitoris under my finger-tip, tongue-tip was then and still is a delight. Sliding my fingers up deep inside her brought that keen cry I'd known was there, waiting to be released. The amazing ring of muscles women have all up and down that magic passage flex for me and for her, tightening, loosening, until everything that's been stored deep within for centuries, it seems, the pain, the fear, the loneliness, the loss, and the joy of rebirth, lets go.

Afterward, she pulls me up, her own scent and flavor, salty, earthy on my lips, easily passed to hers – and the dance goes on.

She likes me to tell her what I want and then give it to me, bring out from me the very same I've asked from her. She wants me sometimes on my knees and elbows, hovering over me from the back, reaching in to slide fingers into my own secret passage. She wants me other times on my back, wide open the way I take her. I see her lovely face between my thighs. She reaches up to tease me. She spans her hand across my breasts, a fingertip on each nipple. She is a lover who knows how to tease til you're ready to burst, then swiftly, with fingers and tongue, to take you home. And so, now, whenever we dance, she says, "I remember that first time, dancing, and I remember when you kissed me in the street."

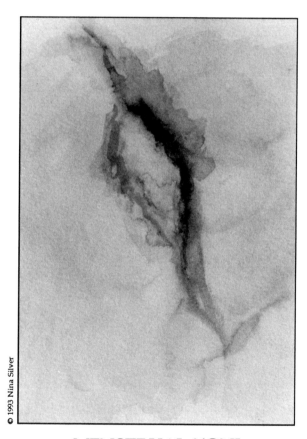

MENSTRUAL YONI

PROLOGUE

Sarah Schulman

Anna sat in the dark as the radio crackled like one emotion too many. Her passion was like sweat without the sweat. It had no idea. No idea of what clarity is. It was two holes burned in the sheet. It was one long neck from lip to chest, as long as a highway. Hot black tar, even at night. A guy spits in the next apartment. There's a dog on the roof.

In Anna's mind they were two scarves, two straps, two pieces of fresh pine wood. How many body parts can a person have? It's unfathomable.

Later, there was a whipping in a hotel room. That woman made her pay a dollar before she let her come. There was sex in a telephone booth, on the pier, in a public bathroom. She kissed her with someone else's pussy on her breath.

Anna walked to the end of the bedroom and looked out the window through the hot iron gates. She walked through the kitchen, dirty linoleum sludging underneath her feet. The cigarette was burning. She opened the front door to see a different kind of light. Someone was coming up the stairs. It was cooler in the hallway. The moon was red through the staircase window.

Up close, that woman looked very different. She was still a princely beauty, but she wore a rough, white, dirty, sleeveless t-shirt like some guy. Her nipples hooked its edges. The hair under her arms was black smoke, wire, a racoon tail, dry polish.

(Excerpted from the novel Empathy.)

MONDAY NIGHT AT THE MOVIES

Lesléa Newman

I'm a girls-just-wanna-have-fun type of gal and so is my best friend, Nancy. When she left the Big Apple for the Pioneer Valley of western Massachusetts, the city just wasn't any fun anymore.

"When are you coming back?" I yelled into the phone one Sunday morning, my left hand cupped over my free ear to drown out the siren wailing up Second Avenue.

"Never," Nancy said. "It's Paradise up here. I know you don't believe me, but there is life after the Rotten Apple."

No, I didn't believe her, but when I lost my job and got mugged all in the same week, I figured I didn't have all that much to lose. So I joined Nancy in what they actually call the Happy Valley, and though the scenery is lovely and the lack of cockroaches divine, well, it's just kind of quiet around here, even for Paradise. I mean, there's just not that much to do for two good time gals like us after 10:00 at night. Or 9:00 for that matter. For a while in December the stores downtown were open until 9:30 and that was kind of exciting. But now it was January and all the holiday cheer was gone, leaving us with inflated VISA bills, single digit temperatures and not much else.

I was browsing through the Saturday paper one afternoon (there is no Sunday paper, if you can believe it) when an ad caught my eye: Movie Extras Wanted. Actors, Actresses, Musicians. No Experience Necessary. I called Nancy immediately. Of course she had clipped the ad, too.

"I can't wait to audition!" I yelled into the phone. "Maybe we'll meet Madonna. Or Cher!"

"I doubt it," Nancy said. "Don't you think they have better things to do than watch a bunch of wanna-be's make fools of

41

themselves at the Springfield Ramada Inn on a Monday night?"

"Maybe they're looking for ethnic faces," I said hopefully: I'm Jewish and Nancy's Italian. We talked on the phone a few minutes longer and decided I would cook us dinner and Nancy would drive. We also decided our chances would improve if we each went as a type and Nancy generously agreed to go frumpy so I could go glamorous. However, when Monday night rolled around and the temperature dropped below my shoe size, I decided to forego my sequined mini-dress in favor of an oversized sweater on top of tight, black leggings. Nancy showed up in an identical outfit and I pretended not to notice that my idea of glamour was the same as her idea of frump.

The ride took about half an hour and as we approached Springfield, our nervousness kicked in. "Do you think we have a chance?" I asked Nancy. "I mean, when I was a kid, this friend of my father's was always saying to me 'You oughtta be in pictures,' but he was just a creep who was always trying to pull me on his lap so he could play with my hair."

"The whole thing might be a scam," Nancy warned me as we pulled off the highway. "One of my co-workers went to one of these once and it turned out to be a recruitment session for a religious cult."

"Oh, great," I groaned, feeling like a fool already. "We'll probably be the only ones there."

Nancy pulled into a parking space and cut the engine. We each fussed with our hair and then stepped out into the wind which totally disheveled us. We ran for the hotel lobby, where a sign that simply said, "Casting" pointed us to the right.

After a quick trip to the women's room to check our lipstick, we rounded the corner and entered a ballroom filled with over two-hundred people of all shapes and sizes. Most of them were dressed to kill, and each of them was filling out a form. I asked a woman who looked like she'd used a magic marker to apply her eyeliner where she got her application. "Up there," she pointed with a number two pencil, "from the lady with the hair."

Nancy and I made our way up to the front of the room where the woman with "the hair" who did not look unlike Dolly Parton gave us an application and told us to get on line for an interview. We moved to the end of the room and I leaned on Nancy's back to fill out the form. Under "name" I put Dolly Grip as Nancy had made me promise not to sign anything. I filled out my address and phone number and pondered the only other question on the application: "Why do you think you can succeed in this business?" "Because I always succeed in everything I do," I wrote, thinking that after all, a movie star should exude confidence. Meanwhile, Nancy filled out her form in bright red lipstick, hoping that would make an impression.

We inched our way to the front of the room. I listened to the interview of the man in front of me, whose cologne was making me dizzy. "Ever acted before?" he was asked.

"Oh, yes," he said. "Shakespeare, Ibsen, Ionesco...."

"Fine, come back tomorrow for a screen test. Next," the interviewer barked, placing his paper to the left.

I pushed Nancy in front of me. The interviewer took her application without looking at it.

"Ever acted before?"

"No."

"Do any public speaking?"

"Oh yes, at my job I...."

"Great, have a seat. Next." He slid Nancy's paper to the right and took my application.

"Ever acted before?"

"No."

"Any musical talent?"

"No."

He made eye contact with me and as far as I could tell was not dazzled by my stunning good looks, as I had hoped. "Are you down here on a lark?"

"Yes," I stammered.

"Have a seat. Next." And he slapped my application down on top of Nancy's.

I sat down next to Nancy and we compared notes. "Why didn't he ask me about public speaking?" I moaned, crossing my legs at the ankles in case anyone was looking. Then I jumped up and made Nancy switch seats with me, since I look better from the right. She rolled her eyes, but humored me. We immediately struck up a conversation with the woman beside Nancy, who it turned out had once been on a local TV commercial. She immediately became the celebrity of our row: a man in front of her turned around to ask her what one should wear to a screen test and the woman behind Nancy leaned forward to listen to her reply. She said basic black was best but a man two seats down said stripes were definitely the way to go if you want to get attention. "Whatever you do, don't wear orange," a woman behind me said. Everyone had an opinion: I hadn't felt this much camaraderie since the last time I was in Manhattan riding a crosstown bus. The man to my left told me he was out of work and could use even a mere twenty bucks a day. "Good luck," I said. "You, too," he answered as we shook hands.

Then a hush came over the room as the man who had interviewed us rose wearily from his seat, grabbed a microphone and launched into his shpeel. He told us that going through a casting agency was the only way to break into the business and then proceeded to explain why this casting agency was the best. He told us that out of all the people sitting in the room, only about four or five had what it took to make it. He explained how hard the work was, and how much money we would need to spend traveling from set to set and printing up copies of our resumés and 8x10 glossies. I slouched down in my seat as he droned on, thinking I missed *Murphy Brown* for this? Finally he rattled off the list of movies they would soon be casting for, in hopes, no doubt, of impressing us.

"But," our host said with a smile, "you know why you're all here, don't you? You're all being considered for *Nazi Lesbians From Hell*."

As the room exploded in laughter, Nancy and I locked eyes: we are both lesbians. Suddenly we were no longer just one of the crowd, out on a lark or perhaps to pursue a dream. Suddenly we were other, feared and hated, the butt of everybody's joke. As people around us continued to chuckle, I felt sweat collecting under my sweater. The man to my left, who'd shaken my hand earlier, smiled at me. I didn't smile back. Would be have been so friendly if he knew? I wondered. Obviously he had no idea he was laughing at Nancy at me. We are both Glamour Dykes and would no sooner leave the house without lipstick than most people would leave the house without their underwear. Consequently, we "pass." I can't speak for Nancy, but I know that ninety-nine percent of the straight people I meet assume I am one of their own, unless I inform them otherwise.

Our presenter continued his prepared speech, but I was no longer listening. Where is ACT-UP or Queer Nation when you need them? I wondered. I looked around the room. If the current statistics were true, then twenty of the two-hundred people sitting in that room were gay. Not to mention the fact that undoubtedly more than a few of us had gay friends, siblings, parents, uncles, aunts, neighbors, teachers, doctors, hairdressers, electricians, etc. etc. Were Nancy and I the only ones who found the presenter's joke unfunny? Had we truly turned into a pair of feminists with no sense of humor?

As our host's endless speech dragged on, I turned the phrase over in my mind. Nazi Lesbians From Hell. Nazi and Hell are synonymous with evil. Am I so vile? I wanted to scream. But I didn't scream. I said nothing.

After telling us for the last time how expensive this venture would be and how only two or three of us would make it, our host read off the chosen few who would appear tomorrow at two o'clock sharp for a screen test. He read off ninety-seven names.

"It's definitely a scam," Nancy whispered to me. "Why would they bother with so many people if only three of us have what it takes to make it?" I shrugged my shoulders; she continued thinking out loud. "They probably charge you for the screen test. Or make you buy one-hundred 8x10 glossies. Or something."

We'll never know, as neither of our names were called. Nor was the man siting next to me, whose smile had been replaced by a look of quiet desperation. The woman next to Nancy beamed and everyone wished her luck.

Nancy put on her coat and turned to me. "Ready?"

"One second," I said, and before I knew what I was doing, I made my way up to the front of the room.

"Excuse me." I stared at our casting director, who was now trying to fit his mike into its stand, like the movie star we all yearned to be.

"Yes?" He smiled and put his hand on my shoulder.

"I'm a Jew...." I said.

"Oy," he interrupted.

"...and," I swallowed hard, "I'm a lesbian, and..." I waited until he finished laughing. "And your joke really offended me."

His hand flew off my shoulder as his face snapped shut. "Listen, doll," he snarled, "this is my show and I'll say whatever the hell I want."

"I'm sure you will," I said. "I just needed to let you know." I walked away as he hurled some words at my back that I couldn't quite make out which was probably just as well.

"What'd you say to him?" Nancy asked as made our way back to the car. I repeated the conversation as we shivered in the front seat, waiting for the engine to warm up.

"Why didn't you tell me?" she asked. I would have gone up with you."

"I don't know. I didn't think about it. I just did it."

"I am so proud of you." Nancy backed the car out of its parking space. "That was so brave."

I tried to shrug it off. "It's no big deal." I stared out the window, thinking. "It'll probably just add fuel to his fire. You know, the next time he says it, he'll probably add, 'and I did meet a Nazi Lesbian From Hell in Springfield, Massachusetts, and boy did she need a good....'"

"Never mind him," Nancy said, steering the car onto the road. "You didn't do it for him. You did it for yourself. For us. For every lesbian in that room. You did it so you could look yourself in the eye and not feel ashamed."

"Oh yeah?" I pulled the rearview mirror toward me as we waited at a red light and stared at my own reflection. What did I see? A Jewish Lesbian From Paradise. "You oughtta be in pictures," I said, and blew myself a kiss.

SAY MY NAME

Karen Moulding

I'm standing by the pool table at the Bar, hands in my front pockets, eyeing my stack of quarters on the ledge, when Anne walks into the room and sits down in a chair behind me. I turn and offer her a tentative smile. She is the cousin of my former friend, Tanya. I say "former" because of what Tanya did on the phone yesterday, telling me I call too much, cancelling her promise to go to court with me the next week, and, the worst, daring to accuse me of worrying too much about the upcoming trial of the man who raped me last fall. "I decided I can't miss a day of work," she said. "Anyway, when are you going to get over that?" These verbal tirades had exploded from her before, and more and more frequently lately. This time, I decided that was it. I'd had it.

Tanya was my first dyke friend in New York. And, to date, she was my only lover for more than one night. But that was several months ago. I'm a professional gymnast, a trainer. Tanya and I met in the aerobics course I was teaching once a week until I found enough New York clients to support myself. We agreed we weren't each other's type, and then promptly hopped into bed. Tanya said she likes them big and butch, and I'm five-foot-three, one hundred pounds. I told her I wanted someone more femmy than her. I'd only recently divorced my husband and come out, chopping off all my hair, sticking the little black skirt in a drawer, and wiping off the lipstick.

I'd been a butch little kid. I had insisted that everyone call me "Andrew," and I pulled on my crotch every night in bed, counting to fifteen, certain this would grow me a penis. Since I came out, I feel more and more butch, like the Andrew I lost somewhere, although there are some who would say I'm not pulling it off, a femme in disguise.

But maybe that's what little Andrew was too. "You were a very bossy kid," said a friend from childhood I recently ran into. She was referring to my favorite childhood game, in which I made her be the teacher, and I was Andrew. I was always bad. "Spank me," I would demand. And she did, over and over, pressing my vagina against her bony knee. Bossy? There's some irony in this. Nevertheless, I stand here now, short-haired, hands in pockets, staring coolly at my quarters and eyeing around the room for big breasts and long hair.

I search Anne's face as I smile tentatively, wondering if she'll even acknowledge me, since I'm no longer friends with Tanya. Not only is Anne Tanya's cousin, she's also the girlfriend of Tanya's oldest friend, Kate. The four of us went bowling once, when I was still in the throes of my fling with Tanya. Anne stood behind Kate, her arms reaching around to show her how to hold the ball. A queer feeling churned in my stomach at that moment, which I still remember. "You show me," pleaded Tanya, grasping my hands. And I hated the sound of Tanya's whine, as well as Kate's shrill giggle. Glancing down at my funny rented green shoes on the shiny blond wood floor, I believed for a second that I stood on a stage, and that both Tanya and her best friend Kate were actresses hired to support me in some role of which I wasn't even aware. I did bowl better than Tanya, though not nearly as well as Anne. And my arms weren't long enough to reach around Tanya's breasts and show her how to do anything.

Anne is a lot bigger than me, fifty pounds and a foot. Tonight she wears a plain green work shirt – which I notice flatters her eyes, faded Levis, and black hiking boots. She slumps back in her chair, as if bored or exhausted. My palms feel damp for some reason, and I wipe them on the front of my jeans.

"You're so butch!" Tanya commented after our first few times. My hands are small, so it was nothing to get my whole fist inside her. "Jesus!" she moaned. And I slapped her until she agreed to say my name. None of this "Jesus" shit around me. So Tanya said my name, then again and again. I felt tall that month. But by the fifth or sixth time, I also felt anxious. How long could I be this tall? Was four inches shorter really tall enough for her? Hitting her harder seemed the only way to make up for my stature, but the thought of inflicting real pain was worse than the thought of having only a fleeting effect on her. We'd always planned to only have a fling anyway, and so it ended.

Anne hasn't moved so, finally, I turn around to speak. "Did you hear?" I ask.

"Hear what?" She yawns.

"About our fight."

"No. Tell me." Something about the way she says this makes me nervous, although not unpleasantly, and I giggle and stutter a bit while I skim through the story.

She shrugs at the end. "You'll make up," she proclaims.

I doubt this, but say nothing.

"So are you and Kate serious and monogamous?" I ask, to make conversation. Tanya had told me that monogamy was already an issue between them.

Anne just shrugs again. "I don't really know her that well," is the response. This surprises me. Anne and Kate have been together for over six months, since just before my fling with Tanya.

"Hey," I say, changing the subject. "So tell me how to pick up a girl."

Anne grins. "Try this," she suggests. "Hey baby, wanna come in the bathroom and make out?"

I repeat the line, sticking my chest out and flexing my bicep. Anne bursts out laughing.

The two beers I drank earlier have gotten to my head and I'm filled with this warm, friendly feeling toward Anne. She'll be my buddy. She's butch like me. "I'm very strong," I say to her, as if confiding something to her, something just between us butches. "I can do five chin ups." Anne's forehead wrinkles and, as she yawns, I think I see her eyeballs roll toward the ceiling. I feel my cheeks glow. Why am I acting so stupid? And why do I care how I'm acting? A desperate nervousness rises.

"This is my best part!" I burst out. I turn around and march back and forth past Anne's chair, pointing to my own ass. "Should I put a sign there, so the girls see?"

Anne just lifts her eyebrows at this.

Somewhere in the conversation, I wonder where Kate is

tonight, but I forget to ask.

"You won't have a problem," Anne mumbles at one point. "You're charming."

This comment strikes me as odd, but I don't have time to think about it now. My quarters are up, and it's time for me to play. My stomach jumps as if I'm going too fast in an elevator. Anne might leave now. I brush aside the thought and, after the winner's break, stand up for my first shot.

How could I mistake the eight ball for the one? I watch paralyzed as the cue ball follows my fatal scratch. How to regain my cool? What look on my face as I turn around?

But there is no turning. Her arm has reached from behind me across both shoulders and I'm leaning back into her frame. Before I can stop it, my eyes close.

"That was a very bad shot," she whispers, the breath warm in my ear. There's a distinct accent on the word "bad." My instant thought is that Tanya told her, told her cousin Anne about my spanking fetish.

But then there are waves on the back of my neck. Her left hand. The room swims and there's no air to think. "Did you ever try this on the girls you try to pick up?" she whispers, the breath hotter now, like steam.

Her right hand drops slightly, grazing my nipple. An accident? When did my tit get so hard? An arrow of arousal shoots past my belly-button down my cunt and I realize she has grabbed my nipple between two fingers through my shirt, pinching it briefly, hard.

I try to think of the correct butch response. A smirk? A giggle? But the noise comes out as a moan.

"That was a bad shot, baby," she repeats. Where did the "baby" come from?

I swallow and nod.

"Come to the bathroom and show me your best part again," she whispers, barely audible.

My clit throbs and my whole crotch contracts. My brain is somewhere else. I grin awkwardly at my pool opponent. No time to shake hands. I forget to swagger as I follow Anne into the small, dark room.

"Good thing there wasn't a line yet," I say, stupidly, when we face each other in the square bathroom.

"Turn around," is her answer. With a flick of the head she gestures toward the wall. Her face is a blank. I'll have to learn how to do that, I think.

"Didn't you hear me?" This time there is a slight sneer, a hint of laughter, in her tone.

I giggle nervously, then turn, leaning my upper arms against the wall, above my head.

"Oh, so *this* is your best part," she says from behind me.

Her hand has slid down past my belt, into my panties. I start from the cold. Or maybe it's from the feel of another's skin against mine, after so many months. She cups my left cheek and squeezes, rolling the flesh among her long fingers. A hum escapes me.

"What's that noise?" comes her whisper against my right ear. "Is that a *butch* noise?" She squeezes on the "butch," and then slides a finger into my crack. Her wrist is stuck by my belt, and so the finger barely reaches my cunt, its tip resting there, at the rear of the hole, not entering. Her thumb grazes back and forth over my anus.

"I asked you a question," she says. The breath in my ear makes my neck drop limp to one side, and somehow her other hand has reached around, unbuckled my belt, and yanked open my fly. She slips that hand into the front of my panties, until a finger dives into my wet hole. Fingers press simultaneously from the front and rear. Spreading me length-wise, the two hands apply even pressure to my clit and ass. I moan again, breath hard, push my pelvis into her palm.

"That noise again," she says, loudly and officiously. Then she leans her mouth into my ear, returns to the whisper. "If you don't answer the question, I'll take off your belt and use it. And *everyone* will hear."

The pressure releases as she pulls out both hands, grabs the sides of my jeans and underwear, and tugs them down to my upper thighs. My ass is exposed and goose bumps fly there. I squeeze my eyes tight against the embarrassment, pray silently that the door is locked.

"Not!" I say quickly.

"That's it," she says, running her fingers up my neck, caressing the base of my skull. "Not what?"

I swallow. "That noise wasn't, uh, butch," I spew out

quickly, then giggle.

"Are you sure it's funny?" she asks slowly, pulling on my belt, sliding it an inch through the loops, then another inch.

"No," I say quickly.

"Good!" she exclaims with mock enthusiasm. She pats my bottom. Then, after a pause, she gives it one hard whack. "That's for the lousy pool," she remarks, a sudden afterthought. A tingling begins where she slapped, creeps down and around to my clit. I writhe, moan again. Her hand slides down my ass and she slips three fingers up inside my wet cunt, then down, then up again. Creating a rhythm, she fucks me like this.

"What else isn't butch, besides that noise?" she asks plainly, not letting up on the rhythm.

I close my eyes again and swallow. Then I say it: "Me."

Slowly she slides out the hand, grasps both my shoulders, and turns me around. As she leans down to kiss my mouth, I'm shocked at the shyness in her green eyes –gems shrouded by soft brown lashes.

"Why do you do it?" she asks. "It's so silly."

"Maybe the attack," I guess. this only occurs to me as I say it. I'm about to dismiss it as an over-dramatic theory when I realize that it's true. Everything that led up to this moment is true, tomboy, marriage, attack, acting butch, and now this. Suddenly aware of the softness of her breast against my cheek, my body melts against her, pressing tight with both arms against her back. "It's been a long time," I remark into her chest.

"Maybe your luck is about to change," she comments, then kisses the top of my head. "You know I have stuff to work out with Kate," she adds. "We might even end up monogamous. So this here is just, a one...you know."

"I know," I say, too quickly, trying to hide the sadness in my voice. At least I feel something, I think. It hits me that if my friendship with Tanya wasn't already down the toilet, it would be now. But even as I think this, I know it was already flushed, and it wasn't my choice. This realization provokes a strange jolt of grief mixed with relief. I'll be even more alone in New York now. But, perhaps, pointed in a more promising direction.

Anne hugs me tighter and already I see that I'll still want her after this, and then I'll hate her for having caused the want. But at this moment that seems a small price to pay. "Hey, you aren't going to leave me like this tonight, are you?" I grin, hoping it distracts from the hurt sheen in my eyes.

She grins back. "Like what?" She peels my t-shirt over my head. "Oh, a little pink bra!" she exclaims.

"Enough!" I say, pressing my palm against her crotch. "I'm not *all* femme. I was a tomboy like everyone else, you know."

"Nobody said you weren't a *dyke*," she says, shoving me gently back into the bathroom corner. The plaster walls are cold against both sides of my bare ass. I'm already dripping wet so she shoves four fingers up me easily. Her other hand unhooks my bra. She leans down and sucks my right nipple, pulling it upward into a hard little rock. Her thumb circles just above my clit, teasing. I rise up on my toes, desperate to meet it, thrusting up.

She lifts her head. "Move for me now," she demands matter-of-factly.

"You're just climbing the walls, aren't you baby?" That whisper again. I thrust harder, higher.

Like a clamp, she pinches my nipple, circles faster and faster with the thumb above my beating clit.

"Yes," I answer. My voice comes out hoarse and deep. At the sound of its strength, I come, thrusting higher and higher upward, toward waves of calm and trembling hope.

© 1993 Nina Silver

DOUBLE YONI

POSTCARDS FROM ANOTHER COUNTRY

Pamela Pratt

"The scenery is great, wish you were here." That's what the first postcard said. "It's a spoof," I explained to people when they saw it taped to a corner of my bathroom mirror. "She would never send something like that for real." They would smile in such a way as to say they didn't get it, and hadn't thought I had such tasteless friends. The fact that it was an in-joke, special only to Mary and me, helped me with the twinge I got every time I saw the card – which I had stuck purposefully, valiantly where I couldn't miss it, so that I would never forget, even for a second, that she was gone.

In general, though, the cards Mary sent me weren't of scenery or buildings or places she had been. We had a kind of contest to see who could find the most beautiful cards with women on them. Every time I bought one to send to her I bought a duplicate for myself, and on the back of mine copied out carefully whatever I'd written to her. To this day I have carefully preserved both sides of the intercontinental dialogue in toto: a collection of correspondence biographers dream of finding in their subject's back drawers. I had in mind the ladies of Llangollen, perhaps, or Gertrude and Alice, or the way Vita and Virginia should have been.

When there were so many cards I could no longer see my face in the bathroom mirror, I transferred the collection to the wall beside my bed, placing her cards and my replies in meticulous order, taped hingelike, the way stamp collectors do, so that I could lift them up and see what she had written on the backside. She had a small, childish handwriting, terrible spelling, and her lines wavered violently across the page.

Mary wrote: *I have an apartment now. I share it with a nice woman Jenny, who is English. I wish she were French, then I would practice the language more. We study photography and practice all day in our little clothes closet that is now our darkroom. We keep our clothes on two chairs. We sit in cafes at night and drink red wine and sometimes the men look at us and then we see them decide not to bother trying. It is very funny when they do this. Jenny and I are always together. I luv you.*

I wrote back: *This apartment is perfect. It is everything you would demand, had you been here to choose it with me. You will have your own room. We could get a cat. There is morning sun, and the philodendron and clivia thrive. I have placed my work table at an angle to the windows so that the light falls directly on it, over my shoulder, for three hours everyday. My paintings are better than ever. I have had one sketch taken on consignment by a small gallery. I send you all my love.*

Mary wrote: *A nice man, Jenny's brother, took me to the Eiffel Tower, but I stayed downstairs. There were tourists. He is only here for a short time. I think of your soft cheek, your touch. I kiss you.*

So in retrospect, I wasn't able to believe that Mary had meant it when her fingers closed around my wrist whenever my hand slid below her waist, because she'd still been pressing herself closer to my body, and her back arched and her mouth became dry until breath rasped in her throat when I touched her small breasts. I was sure she meant 'yes', that her 'no' was only a vestigial reflex, something she had been taught that I would learn to undo, because her 'no' would slip from its mooring always just long enough for her to get what she came for, what, finally, she could not do without, and then the word would form again on her lips, distinctly this time, not drawn out in a long quavering sigh, and she would right her skirts and tamp down her hair and be gone.

I was busy second guessing Mary, so sure I knew what she *really* wanted, no matter what she said, and then chiding myself on how politically incorrect it was not to take a woman at her word. That every *other* word out of her mouth was a kind one confused me, gave me hope, kept me there.

Mary wrote: *Jenny tells me it is all right on the Continent for women to walk arm in arm. She has pointed out to me many women like this, and I see how no one ever looks at them twice. So if you visit me here we will walk hand in hand down the Seine. I kiss you.*

My bedroom wall was covered with the beautiful women: I felt them watching over me as I faded into sleep at night, and had the illusion they all bore Mary's face. I felt comforted, watched over. She is really here, I would think, next to me. She is as close as can be.

Mary wrote: *I met a man; he is very nice. He took me to Versailles to see a palace. It is so beautiful I will never leave here, no matter what it takes. This will be my home and you will visit. I am happy. I miss you.*

Sometimes when I lifted this card I would see only "I met a man" and I would be cranky and miserable all day long; other mornings my eye picked out "I miss you" and I would set out to conquer the world. I understood it was not healthy that the weather of my days was dictated by what had been written weeks before by a woman thousands of miles away.

When I met Maria, Mary had been gone for eight months. "I hope all those cards aren't from the same person," Maria said coolly, the morning after the first evening we slept together at my apartment. "Souvenirs? Or just the ghosts of chance, perhaps." She wasn't posing the kind of question that requires any answer, and the way she threw the comment at me, over her shoulder while she brushed her teeth at the kitchen sink, I knew she had sneaked a peak at the backsides of at least some of the cards. Before I invited her over again, I taped down the bottom edges so she couldn't read the other side.

There was an empty place in my life that Maria seemed to fit beautifully, and in my mind there was also a place where it seemed to me Maria and I would naturally conclude our relationship: on the doorstep of the ivy covered cottage Mary and I would occupy happily to our dying days. I was waiting steadfastly for Mary to come home, amazed and impressed by how true I stayed to her in my heart. I was learning how to cook, I was learning how to love and make love and be insidiously tender. What I did with other women didn't count, because it was all for Mary. I saved all of it for her, wasted nothing on my mentors. I was twenty: fresh footed, anxious, proud. I was striving to be tough and jaded and Maria was already there and trying to step down from it a bit. We met somewhere in the middle of who we were and what we were trying to project, and I hadn't yet learned there was a difference between the over and the under of it. I was passing time with Maria, I was moving slow but on my way somewhere else when I met her, obsessively in love with a girl who told me she loved me, but only in postcards from another country.

Maria never said words like 'love', she said 'fuck', she said 'Fuck me,' – loudly, softly, all the time. I wasn't able to perceive it as only a stylistic difference, see that Mary and Maria might be saying the same thing, or that Maria's version might be more truthful or even preferable in the long run.

Maria demanded to be touched. Her body deserved it. She didn't deny love or lust or any of the subtleties in between I was used to skimming over just to get by with Mary. Maria was proud of her large breasts, the way they swung in her loose t-shirts when she walked, independent of her gait and of each other, like small creatures on short leashes, with minds of their own. She was only twenty five, but her breasts had dropped as though she had been through many years and many children. Instead, she had been through many men and then even more women, lumbering through them the way an express train slows its speed going through a town without ever, ever stopping. In spite of this, there was still something tentative about her when I met her, as though she were truly discovering love for the first time.

When I lay down to make love with Maria my breasts slid off my chest and disappeared into the pockets of my armpits. She laughed at me for wearing a bra and when I told her my breasts hurt otherwise, she laughed even more. "That's something your mother taught you to scare you into being proper," she said. "Your breasts are too small to matter." She thought bras were incorrect, a vestigial remnant of the tyranny of corsets and men, and I stopped wearing them, afraid to be outdone on some political front, however remote it might be.

But when she raised her skinny body above mine, holding my hands down to my sides, and her heavy breasts grazed my flat breast bone, teasing me, I wasn't only twenty, I was everything she had ever done or known, and I wasn't thinking about Mary then, I wasn't learning this for Mary anymore. Her breasts would fall heavily against my cheeks, drifting across my face, first one and then the other as she swayed back and forth above me, mischievous, daring, courting coaxing. My teeth would finally close on a nipple in exasperation and that insistence, meeting her demand, would cause her to drop them, one by one, as though she had dozens of breasts to spare, into my mouth. Moans would rise then, from the back of her throat, from somewhere way behind or beyond her, and escalate as she offered her breasts and her body to me, and freed my hands to do what she had willed them to. She shared an apartment with six other people on Avenue B, and to reach her mattress we had to climb over three beds in a loft area so close to the ceiling you couldn't even sit up. She pretended to never notice the audience we had, and I thought it was a political imperative not to mind. Sometimes my eyes would flick open involuntarily in the moment before orgasm, and I would find myself staring into the glowing eyes of a stranger, who would disappear in the pain of delight.

Maria was the ticket taker in a porno movie house on the east side. I would pick her up at midnight, after the box office had closed, and we would slip into the back of the theater and watch the last show. Everything I know about porn I know from watching those shows and the men who came to see them. Maria knew the names of the stars and the length of their cocks and she knew people who knew people who knew whether they were straight or gay, and what they really liked off stage. She liked having sex while she whispered these things to me in the back of the theater, although sometimes we'd get outside and she'd push me into a phone booth and slide me up against the door. We'd walk home down Third Avenue, stopping in Blarney Stone bars for shots on the way. Maria riled easily and we would fight over nothing, the old men at the bar taking sides and spurring us on, or else, drunk and maudlin, begging us not to break up over nothing.

I couldn't afford my apartment, and had a roommate who slept in what would be Mary's room, a roommate I considered disposable and who's tenancy I could terminate the moment Mary was home for good. My roommate was straight, and I liked to tell people that to show I wasn't prejudiced about people's sexual orientation. I mentioned her so much, in fact, that when Maria and I first met she assumed my roommate and I were lovers. My roommate was so obviously straight that that interpretation didn't occur to me: when Maria actually met the woman she changed the scenario in her mind to me being hopelessly in love with a straight woman. She asked me, and I denied it vehemently. But I thought it was adult and kinder to show the substantive truth of my emotions, if not their object, and so did purposely brutal, casual things to let her know I had allegiances and prior commitments to other women. In the face of her coolly contained jealousy I continued to say we did this, did that, we're planning on this or that, overplaying my relationship with my roommate, or even throwing in the names of women I might or might not ever see again.

I planned a big bash for my twenty first birthday, inviting everyone I had ever even talked to, and went around to my elderly neighbors and explained politely that there might be a little noise come Saturday night. People floated in and out, brought bottles of champagne or tabs of acid--these were the kind of stylistic differences I could understand--and their contributions kept the party going way after our wine ran out, all the way to the Staten Island ferry, in fact, to watch the sunrise.

Somewhere in the middle of the night Mary walked into the party unannounced. I hadn't even known she was in the country. Our party had extended out into the hall: she walked through the crowd of people with a stately, assuming grace as though the Red Sea were parting for her. She dropped her suitcase on the floor and we moved into an embrace that turned into a close dance as the music, changed, as if preordained, to something slow. The party closed back in on us: we were alone. Later, when we broke apart, and Mary had merged with the party, Maria pulled me silently, angrily, farther down the hall to where we could be alone. "Who is she?" she demanded.

"Someone I used to know."

"She's the one you're in love with."

Avoiding her eyes, I found myself staring at the poster on my neighbor's door: a black light chart of zodiac signs, each sign complete with a lesbian couple in a different sexual position. The neighbor was a pimp, and while he walked the streets of the village all night long with his two Dobermans straining at their chains, we could hear the sounds of satisfaction his women made, that the men had paid to hear. He would follow me at night sometimes, spooking the women I brought home from the gay bar around the corner, or from the after-hours club next door. I was so used to him that I no longer perceived him as a possible threat: at most I blanked him out of my mind. Now, I looked closely at the pictures, wondering if I had accomplished every one of them: I had a photographic memory for that sort of thing.

"Why don't you deny it?" Maria asked furiously, after giving me a moment to reply.

I shrugged my shoulders at her. "You want me to say she's only a friend? What do you want me to say? I'll tell you anything you want."

"I want you to tell me the truth."

"No, I don't think you do. I think you want me to love you – I'm sorry – I didn't realize that before."

"You fuck. You asshole." She ran down the stairs and I could hear the reverbations of the glass in the front door after she slammed it shut.

"Maria." But I called her name only after I was sure she was gone. I stood there, not thinking a thing, until I felt fingers running through my hair, and lips on my neck.

"Who was she?" Mary asked softly.

"Someone I used to know."

"Do you want to go after her?" Mary's arms were around my waist, pulling me back into her. I put my hands on her hips and locked her to me and we stood like that for a while, as though there were really a decision to make.

I turned around to her, finally, and said, "You came home for my birthday. Thank you. There isn't anything you could have done that would be more wonderful than that."

"To tell the truth, I forgot it was your birthday. I came here tonight because my plane was so late I missed my train to Boston. And anyway, it's probably better I tell you in person."

"What's in Boston?" I asked, bewildered.

"The man I'm going to marry," she said. She was actually smiling at me. "Aren't you going to wish me the best and all that? We're going to live in Paris for years and years. He's promised me." She stood there with her arms still circling me, her lips an inch from mine, as though she were leaning in for a kiss while she whispered these things to me.

"Oh, well, if he's *promised* you, that makes all the difference, doesn't it," I said mockingly. Totally in control. Either this isn't happening at all and the acid did get dropped in the wine, I thought, or it's real and I'm going to pull it off just fine.

"He's very rich," she said, and then caught herself, and added, "Not that that means anything."

"Did you sleep with Jenny?" I asked quickly.

"Why do you always want to know things like that for," she said, dismissing the question with a wave of her hand.

The room was tilting and I had to let Mary go to hold myself upright against the wall. I decided it wasn't worth the effort of keeping up the pretence that what she had just said didn't have a whole other meaning for me.

"Why do you come here? What did you think telling me in person would accomplish? I mean, you can't not know," I said, "It isn't possible." I could hear my words coming from another corner of the hallway, distinct, separate, spaced widely apart, and spoken in a voice totally unlike mine. "So it suddenly seems quite clear to me that that must be *why* you come here. Why you keep seeing me, writing me – egging me on. What do you get out of watching me fawn over you, ache for you, wait for you?" All along I had thought I would finally win Mary over by the intensity of my passion, but this foolishness evaporated suddenly, leaving me empty. I was abandoned: not by Mary, whom I had never had, but by my own hopes and dreams. "You must get off on it," I said, but it came out lame and washed out. I couldn't even fake fury with her, I didn't even have that much left.

"I came here because I love you," she said. "Just because I will never live with you, never love you in the way you want, doesn't mean I don't love you in my own special way. You of all people must understand how impossible it would be for me to live that kind of life."

"You mean as the social pariah you seem to think being a lesbian entails?"

"Of course my family would never speak to me again if they knew," she said. "But there's no reason they *would* ever have to know," she continued soothingly, "not if you don't make such a big deal out of it." Here she had the grace to hesitate for just a second. "We'll keep in touch. I'll have to fly into New York to see Mother occasionally, so it's not like we'll never see each other again." She watched me intently to see how I was taking this, and then when she saw my eyes go wide open and fix upon her face, with all the anger I had tried to conjure up before blossoming suddenly, Mary leaned in to initiate the kiss I had been waiting aeons for, and had only a moment before given up on, but it was only to cut off my chance of reply.

"The most erotic kiss I've ever seen in my life," someone at the party said to me later. "I was coming out to wish you a happy birthday, but no way was I going to interupt *that*."

"But I can see I won't be able to stay here tonight," Mary said, quickly putting the kiss back in what she considered its proper perspective, in case her ardor had gone to my head. "Not with all these people. This party could go on for hours. It was a long plane ride, and I need some sleep. I'll find somewhere else to crash, don't worry."

"I'll send them away," I said. All I heard was that she had been intending to spend the night with me. A last night – a send off, I thought. Make it a proper one. And that's why the party ended up on the Staten Island ferry – so that Mary and I could be alone. I wasn't interested in watching the sunrise: I was sitting in a corner of my room, watching Mary sleep, saying goodbye to her silently. She had gone to bed with an armor of lacy white underwear just visible beneath a shapeless t-shirt, as though she thought I would try to take advantage of her while she was asleep. I thought about it seriously and dismissed it, but not because it was macho and disrespectful: conquest as a theoretical idea wasn't as completely repellent to me as I would have liked it to be. But any anonymous body in my bed would have produced a greater response in me than what I felt for Mary that night. I didn't want her if I couldn't have her again and again and again. Sex with Mary was an expression of love, a promise. I had to admit, finally, that that was all it was, that making love to Mary had none of the fervor, the appreciation, of all those other bodies I had touched. Maria for example. It was the great political distinction brought to life, of making love *with* someone or only *to* them.

In the morning, after Mary had left to catch her train, I called Maria. "I'm surprised you had the nerve to call me," she said.

"So what do you want?"

"I'm sorry I hurt your feelings," I said. "I misjudged the situation."

"Which one?" she said crisply.

"Both, I guess." We stayed silent for a while.

"Calling to say you're sorry is a *totally* futile gesture, but how like you to think of it."

Until I had heard her voice just then, I had no idea how fond I was of Maria. "I'll miss you," I said lamely.

"Is this some sort of exercise in manipulation?" Maria said. "Because I'm not falling for it."

"No, I mean it, I'll be lonely without you."

"There's always the other one, or did you screw that up, too?"

"Mary's gone to Boston," I said plaintively. "To a man," I added. "So it was all for nothing."

"You know," Maria said, "I'm really glad you called today. I really am. "Because this is the closest I'll ever get to your face again and I just want to tell you to fuck off. Just fucking fuck off." There was a dial tone after that.

About a week later I got a hastily scribbled note from Mary saying that they hadn't been "able to wait", had gotten married on the spot, and were heading straight back to Europe for their honeymoon. The note was folded around a picture of the two of them together. The man had a red carnation in his lapel, but his features were indistinct because the picture was slightly out of focus and blurred, as though they had moved just as the shutter had clicked. But Mary, because I knew her features, because I had loved her, was clear as day. From one hand she dangled a red rose, with ribbons wrapped round the stem protecting her from the thorns. The flower pointed down toward the ground and I imagined I could discern, though dimly, its petals already shedding onto the steps of the municipal building. Mary waved at the camera with her free hand, in a manner that reminded me of the gesture president's wives make to the press as they step from Air Force One.

In the same mail there was a postcard from Maria. She didn't sign her name to the card, but the content was signature enough. *The scenery is here, wish you were great.*

BREAKFAST

Cody Yeager

Daybreak. I can't sleep any longer, though my body is still exhausted. Sensing that I am awake, my dogs crowd around me, snorting and snuffling like piglets. Tails moving in circles like helicopter blades, they step all over the bed, dislodging the cat who voices his opinion as he glides away. Even though I am surrounded by furry love, my bed feels empty and I jump up, anxious to flee from morning loneliness.

But it's waiting for me; it's there when I run my hairbrush through thick tangles. The loneliness lurks in my toothpaste tube; the fennel taste reminds me of mornings when I didn't wake up alone, mornings when I couldn't wait to wake up. I loved the action of falling asleep, looking forward to a shared breakfast in the morning. The dream of waking up like that for years to come. Inexhaustible energy.

But the trouble with dreams, you see, is that eventually one must wake up. I don't know just why.

This morning, I pull on my jeans while the dogs wait for their walk. The sight of my rumpled sheets freezes me like an arctic blast. After she left us, after the reindeer flannel was soaked with our tears, we gathered up those soft sheets. We buried our stained muzzles in their scent. And then we made a bonfire. Gasoline blended with the scent, sending red-orange skyscrapers to meet the moon's mocking gaze. I hate remembering myself then, an origami soldier collapsed in the rain. The blades of grass cut me like knives. My dogs stood warily by : tails down, ears flattened, panting. Looking at me, their soft eyes asking the unanswered question: How should we feel?

And as I lay there, hating the moon, I could hear myself

outside myself screaming at the starshine: How should I feel? A fistful of earth flung at the sullen moon. No answer.

I look out the window and reach for leashes, glaring at the weather. Rain again. Cold winter rain, just in time for Saint Nikolaus day. My dogs and I prance slowly along the wet streets. As we come to the park, the leashes are snapped off and away they go, leaping and snapping at each other. They slip and slide on the grass and I find myself laughing. The sound startles me; a paper soldier in the rain, the sound frightens me. And then I'm crying, a familiar sound, and paws are all over me, muzzles poking, searching for a cause.

But I don't know anymore what the cause is.

Home again, I mix Purina and a little warm milk while elevated noses sniff expectantly. Watching them eat their breakfast gives me more joy than anything else these days, makes me feel needed. When the bowls are licked clean, they come to me smiling, tails wagging. We are all smiling now, rolling across the floor, books falling everywhere. Suddenly, ears stand up. Suspended animation. The mail drops through the slot and there's a dull thud. A package.

A Saint Nick's day present from my mother. I recognize that copybook handwriting. She never forgets. When we were children, we'd put our shoes on the porch that special evening, carefully clearing away the snow first. In the morning, they were filled with wonder: candy, a little book of verses, tiny bottles of J_germeister, a tiny figurine, Lifesavers. You never knew just what, but that was part of the magic. We'd sleep while Nikolaus went through the still streets, leaving magic. We left the porch light on so he'd be sure and find us. He always did.

Christmas carols are playing on the radio as I pour Sumatran into a mug. Inside the box is my childhood, perfectly wrapped. My mother must have known it would arrive at breakfast time because there is a huge slice of white fruitcake. I know by the smell that it's from K_mmer's bakery on Smithfield Street. Just on the edge of the strip district, you know – beside Devando's fruit stand. There are two bananas for me, dried apricots, and some dates rolled in sugar – only a few of those. They are my father's favorite; I know that when my mother went to get a roll of tape he grabbed a handful at the last second.

But that's not all there is in the box. A small bottle of Goldwasser for a special occasion and a tiny locket with a perfect Edelweiss blossom under glass. And at the very bottom of it all is a red, white, and brown box with a picture of a yellow bowl and a white spoon on the front. I haven't seen a box like that in at least fifteen years, but I know it as I knew my mother's handwriting. Coco-Wheats. The only cereal I would eat. She remembered.

Coco-Wheats, Coco-Wheats, can't be beat, the creamy hot cereal with the cocoa treat....

Every morning, my big brothers would demand their Wheaties. Big orange box with some athlete on the front. My sisters would have eggs and toast. Daddy would come home from the mill just as we were sitting down at the table, all clean and shining in our school uniforms, collars and ties straight, shirts white as chalk. He would not demand anything at all, just eat whatever was there. And me, I'd wait for the water to boil so I could have my Coco-Wheats. My mother made them just right: no lumps and just the right amount of fresh cream, warmed up first so it wouldn't cool off the cereal. Just right.

Then we'd gather up our school things and put on our oxblood colored loafers. Five pairs of them waited by the door, exactly alike except for the sizes. And five leather schoolbags, jammed full. On Sunday morning after Mass, we'd all sit down and put saddle soap on our shoes and bags. My father would help too; we'd huddle around him, rubbing creamy soap into the leather, and he would tell us about his childhood. Nobody sent him to school each morning with a good breakfast in his stomach. He never learned to read; he learned to work in a coal mine. But when he was sixteen, a ceiling caved in and his friend Salvatore was trapped. Daddy could hear him screaming: Aiuto, presto, mio dio presto ! By the time they dug him out, he was dead, rosary in his hand, looking up, waiting for the Holy Virgin to release him. Ave Maria.

That's when my father decided to leave the mines and go to work in a steel mill. Steady work, all night long, for forty good years. We would listen to his stories, interrupting now and then to ask what Daddy thought were stupid questions. Like what's "presto" mean – I thought it meant magic – but Daddy shook his head, saying "You know, presto, presto – like when you're late for work. And my mother answered from the kitchen – It means schnell. Oh, schnell. Hurry up."

Schnell, presto, hurry up. They ran together in our minds, meaning the same thing. Like: Wolfgang = dog = Hund-cane. Made sense to me. My mother always capitalized her word for dog, but when I did that at school with our word for dog, it always came back circled in red. And so did cat, fence, book, and a whole lot of other words. I never told my mother. In time, I figured out that even though the nuns said my mother was wrong to capitalize her words, she wasn't wrong at all. It was just her way. Daddy wouldn't have understood at all. He didn't know what it meant to make some letters big and some small. When he wrote his name, it was always big letters, carefully drawn by a pen tightly gripped in his strong hand.

When our loafers and bookbags were all soft and clean, my mother would quietly announce: "Fr_hst_ck." And we'd jump up, chorusing "Breakfast, breakfast." It never failed; somehow, just as we'd be washing up, a knock would come at the door, or no knock would come and the door would just open. And in would pile Daddy's friends. Sunday morning meant three things to them: no work, Mass, and breakfast at our house. I don't know if my mother ever actually invited them; they just showed up.

Their wives were glad to be rid of them for a while, so in they would come with some contribution to breakfast, wearing their best clothes. Johnny Ciccolini always brought some fresh baked bread from his wife's oven or some special stromboli. We loved that stromboli; it was sort of like a Nikolaus day present because you never knew from week to week what would be wrapped up inside the dough. Banjo Catanese would bring a bottle of sweet wine to sip after breakfast, and Mick Orgadovchec always brought a pound of coffee beans for cappuccino. Sometimes, one of my mother's brothers would drop in too, but they never brought anything. Their wives were relieved to have Sunday to themselves, so they were happy to send these treats along. I guess it seemed like a small price to pay. But they didn't need to send anything at all. My mother loved the company of men. She never asked about any of the wives; she wasn't interested in their lives. Our house was not small, but with all of Daddy's friends it seemed full. Not crowded, just full, just right. They'd all crowd around the table, eating and laughing, the aroma of coffee and Old Spice filling our kitchen. Anything my mother served was exactly what they had all been wanting for breakfast that morning. It was always delicious and there was always plenty of it. She never seemed to run short of anything, even though nobody ever knew how many people would show up.

My favorite time came after breakfast. Mick brewed more coffee and then they would talk. You didn't have to ask them for a story. It seemed like the story of their lives was their lives. My uncle Paul told the story of how our mother's family came from home. It made me wonder where home was, if this wasn't it. My mother always listened carefully to that story. No matter what she was doing, she'd stop and listen. I almost thought I saw tears in her eyes sometimes, but that couldn't be. I liked that story too, but the very best was the one my father would tell about how he came to live in America himself. It was his favorite story to tell, I think; it was his life, after all. It was our favorite story to hear, because like my uncle Paul's story, it was our story too. I still hear it each time I speak or see my face reflected in a mirror. It's my story too.

On the sunny shores of Sicily, where lemon and olive trees meet the sea, stands the great city of Palermo. Daddy would always start the story this way, no matter how many times he told it. When we asked him to skip that part, he'd say: you got to begin at the beginning. 1926, that's the beginning. That's when a handsome young man with the world on a string met a pretty and poor girl walking by the sea. It didn't matter that his family already had a fine girl chosen for him, far away in Catania – a good way to unite two influential families on the big island. It didn't matter that he would be going to Italia soon on family business.

It didn't matter; she loved him.

He was a smooth dancer, light on his feet, dark eyes flashing. He could play the piano too, singing softly – Tu se l'_nica d_nna per me. They knew of course that his family would not approve. At all. So after the music ended, when they sat whispering in his shiny black Fiat, they made their plans. California. He knew people who had emigrated. They could go, they could do it. As soon as he came back from Calabria, they would do it.

Maybe he didn't know he would be gone for a year.

When the doctor told her it was true, she was pregnant, she trembled. Seventeen years old, barely five feet tall, and very thin. Did the father know? No. Who was he, did she know? Did she know? The doctor had been present at her birth, so she told him: Benasi Natale Carabello. After she left the office, messengers were sent to the big house overlooking the harbor. Giuseppia made arrangements for her son to leave for the mainland the next morning – urgent business. So off he sailed. His brothers waved him off and then they went looking for her.

But she couldn't be persuaded. Her father wouldn't listen either, until he suddenly lost his job on the boats. Neighbors stopped visiting. By the time the beautiful baby boy came along, there was nothing in the house to eat but dried bread and cheap wine. Not an easy birth, no doctor came. He would be the only child she was capable of bearing. But what a child: wavy black hair, round cheeks, and his father's eyes. She held him close, very close, but every mother falls asleep sometime. She didn't hear the knock at the door, but when her father came to her bed with a gentleman in a suit and a nurse, she was instantly awake. And screaming. Her father held her down while they pried the baby from her weak arms. It was a relief when she fainted.

The year was 1927. Years later, they would see each other again.

The baby sailed to America with the nurse who promptly disappeared. They should have travelled by train to Sacramento, where a family would pick him up. It was all arranged. But the sight of the mighty woman in the harbor lifting her lamp beside the golden door was too tempting. After the ordeal in the Great Hall of Ellis Island, the nurse put the child on a train to Pittsburgh. Then she got off the train and disappeared in the huddled masses yearning to breathe free.

His trip to the mainland finally over, Benasi came home. His brothers told him about his mistake. His mother sat him down and told him the date of his wedding. He sent his fiancee flowers and went to see the woman he loved. Was California still in the back of his mind? She refused to see him, in fact, never spoke to him again. He had disappeared for a year when she needed him. For a year. He raged, called her cruel, and drank all night. And the next morning, like a good son, he put on a clean suit and went to his wedding.

And then what happened, Daddy? Then what happened? As if we didn't know.

A drunken coal miner sat in a bar in the dusty city of Pittsburgh. Recently arrived there from down the Monongahela in West Virginia. His sickly wife was complaining. On the way home, on the wrong streetcar, he saw a sign: Children's Home. "I want a boy!" he cried. And he walked out with one that had just arrived, the paperwork not even finished. Not that there was any information to fill in. So he walked out with him. Just like that. He walked out with him. And two months later the sickly wife died and was followed by a series of women.

Some of them married the coal miner and some of them didn't.

Moving from mine to mine, there was no time for an unwanted boy to learn to read.

That was my father's welcome to America.

One Spring day, Daddy looked in the mirror and didn't recognize the man who looked back. He took some money from his account at the credit union. There was a burglary down on Wood Street at the Pittsburgh Children's Home, followed by a similar break in a week later at the state capitol's records office. More money from the credit union and Daddy was on a plane to Italy. A boat across to Sicily, a visit to the consulate, a name given: Carabello, and soon he was knocking on a door in a narrow street, his hand trembling.

He only said one word – Mama? But only one word was needed, years later. Mama.

And that was how we learned that we had a grandmother all our own. Living alone in Palermo. Almost every day, she saw Benasi and his wife. He drank every day of his life and sent her flowers on her birthday. Every year, she sent them back. And he kept drinking until it killed him. And it finally did.

My grandmother went to the funeral of the man who sang to her. She pushed her way past his brothers and his wife and she stood beside him for a long moment. Then she walked away, her spit staining his cheek.

Banjo and Mick were always in tears by this time. And all of us would say, come on, Daddy, don't stop there. But he would wipe his eyes and say – you got to end at the ending. That's the end of the story. Finish your breakfast.

Dogs crowding me, I pour boiling water on my Coco-Wheats and I know this is not the end of the story. It's my story too. And this is not the end, I think as I eat my breakfast, this is not the end of the story.

REDHEADS

Sally Bellerose

I'm a sucker for a flashy readhead. Cherry has bucket seats, four on the floor, dual exhaust, and moves when you ask her to. She's getting old, driven just about every day for over twenty years. I know how she feels, so I pamper her.

Charlene's a pretty readhead, too. The red hair is recent, but the rest of her, painted lips, big breasts, big hands, they've been the same since I've known her. Charlene works hard. She moves when she's damn good and ready. Sometimes she lets me pamper her. Sometimes she pampers me.

We're lying on the bed with the moss green sheets in the Jungle Romm of the Pines Motel. The desk clerk didn't blink when we checked in. Two women spending the night together doesn't interest him as much as a rerun of McHale's Navy. There are life-sized cheetahs on the wallpaper, chasing each other around the room. Charlene has been calling me Tarzan all night. When I remember, I call her Jane – but that's my mother's name and life is confusing enough, so I forget.

Charlene hasn't decided yet if she's my girlfriend or not. She's got a lot on her mind. She works as a waitress three nights a week and goes to Community College during the days. She hasn't declared a major yet. Charlene's almost forty. She's at an undecided stage of her life. Not that she's a wishy-washy type of person. She just makes her own decisions in her own time.

We're rolling around in bed and I say, "Charlene, whose girl are you?" Like you might say in the ear of the woman you are lying on top of, while she's got a hand full of you. Most women

---

would say "Yours Baby", if not from passion, at least from habit or politeness.

Not Charlene. She says, "I don't know honey, it's too soon to tell." She goes right on moving her hips and groaning. I try to be cool, but it hurts my feelings. I've got to wonder what all this fucking is about. I've been around the block a few times and there's been more than one woman I've been undecided about myself, but we've been doing this every Tuesday and Friday night for months now. It's not too soon for me to tell. Charlene wants a better life, she's just not sure I'm going to be in it. I suppose I should be happy that she's being honest with me, but I feel like this is some kind of test drive. What can I do? I'm crazy about her. She's got the wheel.

There's another problem with this arrangement. I'm getting tired of this motel. It's exciting at first, but it gets old. We've been in the Jungle Room nine times. There's a trapeze in here, a trampoline, too. You only need a two-foot bounce straight up to reach the trapeze, then it's a pretty limp swing. It's like sex, sometimes the idea of it is more exciting than the actual ride. Charlene's got plenty of extras. We don't have to be wasting our hard earned money on all this equipment.

We're here because I live with my mother. My mother is old. Shit, I'm old. My mother would like Charlene. Charlene is a lady, respectful, unless she's mad. My mother would like her, but I guess I'd better find out if Charlene's my girlfriend before I bring her home. It doesn't break my mother's heart that I'm this way anymore, but she wants to see me in a steady relationship before she dies. I'm trying.

We can't go to Charlene's place because her husband is there. That's how we met, through her husband. I'd say husband is the wrong word. That's what Charlene calls him. They lived together for a few years, like husband and wife. Now they just live together.

His name is Dave. I ran into him one day when he was waiting for Charlene outside of K-Mart. I pulled into the parking space next to him. Cherry was shining red, still wet from the car wash.

"Nice car," he said.

"Thanks," I said.

"69?" he asked.

I nodded yes, got out and locked Cherry up before heading toward K-Mart. He tried to start up his car, planned to have a quick one at the bar across the street. His engine wouldn't turn over. It was July, getting hot. Dave thought it was overheated, but I could tell it was the battery.

"Want a jump?" I asked, unlocking Cherry's trunk and grabbing the cables. Before he got his jump, he started talking cars. He said he loved Mustangs. Cherry's a Mustang. He couldn't get over her paint job or her interior. Wanted to buy her. I could see by the way he took care of his Impala that he wouldn't maintain her. Besides, I wouldn't sell Cherry.

We decided we needed a beer more than the Impala needed a jump. We walked over to the bar. He left a note for Charlene. It was a small note written on the back of a book of matches. It said "Next door" with an arrow pointing across the street. He stuck it under the windshield wiper.

The note was too short and the beer was too long. About an hour later, Charlene walked through the side door of the bar – pissed off and pushing a shopping cart full of K-Mart. She pushed the cart right over to our table and started unloading.

"Your shirts..." she said and plunked six flannels in front of Dave "...three for twenty dollars. Your toilet paper..." she plunked down 30 rolls one at a time "...ten bucks." Then she piled a few cans of mixed nuts, some cleaning stuff and a TV Guide next to him on the bench, pricing as she went. She slid into the booth on my side and hoisted the real prize onto the table. "And one battery – $39.77 on sale – for one shit head."

Then she turned to me and said, "At least my husband chose a good-looking woman to leave me alone for, with a ton of his stuff and in the boiling sun."

She was stretching her points. It was hot, but not boiling, nobody has ever called me a good-looking woman and, like I say, Dave is not really her husband. She was right to be pissed, though. We should have waited for her.

So, it's six months later and here I am lying next to Charlene in the Jungle Room again. She sits up in bed and says, "Baby, I've made up my mind."

I say, "Huh, what are you talking about?" My voice wasn't what you'd call gentle. It was five o'clock in the morning. We'd had a nice night, but we didn't get here 'till midnight and when you're in a sixty dollar room with a trampoline, you tend to bounce around on it whether it's still a kick or not. So I was tired.

She says, "We belong together."

I say, "Yeah, we do," and roll over, hoping she'll do the same.

She shakes my shoulder, says "Come on, wake up, honey. I want to go to confession."

I figure she means this literally, since we're not in the room with the altar and candles. I have mixed feelings. The "Baby...we belong together" part feels good. The confession part feels like trouble.

"What do you need to confess?" I ask.

"Us," she says.

I'm surprised to hear this since, the very first time we met in that bar, Charlene explained to me that the Bible doesn't have a thing to say about women sleeping together. At first, I thought it was just her way of flirting and pissing Dave off. I suppose it was all of that, but she also meant it sincerely, as a point of faith. I'm not religious, myself, but I've got an aunt on my father's side that's a stone butch and she's a nun in good standing. Like Charlene says, the Church doesn't care as long as you don't go around bragging about it.

I say, "Honey, go to sleep. There's no sin in sex. Jesus loves you. I love you."

She says, "Don't be conceited. It's not just you. I've got a husband."

This husband stuff again. Charlene is honest, but she's prone to dramatics. It gets on my nerves. I say, "Come off it, Charlene. You didn't have a church ceremony and you've got no license, so you don't have a husband."

She says, "God knows we were married."

I say, "For Christ's sake." Which wasn't nice, because she really is upset and wants to do right religiously. I roll over. Charlene listens to all my problems, takes a real interest. I should do the same for her. I just wish she would wait until nine o'clock like usual. I sit up in bed meaning to apologize, but that kind of thing comes to me slowly. Before I can say a thing, she's hooking her bra around her waist and hoisting it up over her breasts in a huff and, before I can pull up my pants, she's out the door. I trip over the trampoline and peek through the mauve curtains. Charlene's leaning on Cherry and searching through the pockets of my jacket, which she grabbed on her way out. She finds Cherry's keys and off they go together – my car for sure and my girlfriend, maybe.

These old cars have big gas tanks and Cherry's is full. They could be gone a long time. They won't find a priest awake at five o'clock in the morning. The saints in heaven are still asleep. For the next couple of hours, I join them.

Now I'm waiting and waiting. It's after ten o'clock. I'm getting nervous. After eleven, you pay for a full extra night. Cherry's got my wallet. It's under her front seat. I hope Charlene doesn't know that. I nod off in the chair by the bed and, thank you Jesus, Charlene and Cherry screech in.

I meet her at the door and say, "You okay, baby?", which is the right thing to say.

She says, "Like you care." But I can tell she's softened up. I glance beyond her, see Cherry safe, parked in her spot. Charlene sits on the bed and takes off her flats. She rubs her feet.

"Where have you been?"

"You bought me breakfast..." she says and hands me my wallet "...then I talked to Father John."

"Confession doesn't start 'till twelve o'clock," I say.

"That's why I went to the rectory, my dear."

I move a little closer since she said "my dear". "He heard confession in his living room?" I ask. I don't think that's kosher.

"No, at the breakfast table. He had to. I told him I was having a crisis of faith. It's his job, after all."

"So are you absolved?"

"Well, I told him about my husband and he said the same as you, no church, no sacrament, no husband. He said my sin was having sex with a man I wasn't married to, but not as big a sin as if we were married and I was having sex with a different man or if I wasn't having sex at all but did get married in the church and got divorced."

"Shit. What did he think when you told him about us? "

"Who cares what he thinks? None of it's any of his business. I just wanted this thing with Dave ended formally. God likes things to be ended formally. It's Father John's job to get messages through to Him."

Charlene looked incredible; her face was glowing and she looked like she'd had ten hours of sleep and really had talked to God.

"So did your message get through?"

"Well sure, I've been gone five hours. Of course I spent a couple of hours of that at Denny's and K-Mart."

"What did you get at K-Mart?" I didn't see a K-Mart bag, but I noticed she was wearing something different under her coat.

She took the coat off and smiled. Leopard skin leotards, some new perfume I can't name. They sell all kinds of things at K-Mart. We're going to end up paying for an extra night. It's okay, we've never been alone in the daytime.

I say, "Charlene, now that you don't have a husband, maybe we can get a place of our own."

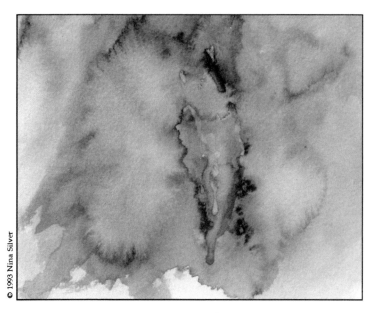

NEBULAR YONI #2

BEYOND SUBMISSION

Sharon Carroll

As if you thought you could touch me there, and then just walk away. As if you thought you could do it – press your body full against mine, part my lips with your tender tongue, run your hand along my breast, my nipple, pushing, pulling, the other hand on my waist, my thigh, moving down, down, slow and sure . . . open that button, unzip the zipper and place your finger there, right *there*, watching me sink back against the wall, my eyes closed, my breathing quick and full . . . you're in charge now, you're in control . . . .

And then, suddenly, you pull away – as if you thought you could do that, turn your back and walk away without a word. No mention of goodbye, no simple salute, no meeting of my eye, no clichéd kiss on the cheek, no silly pleasantry, no fumbling for an excuse, no mumbling of a false apology – yes, nothing more sure, more certain than the back turned, the footsteps receding, the door snatched open, then quickly closed, not slammed, but firmly shut, the sound of footsteps on the stairs, down the stairwell, away . . . . As if you thought you could do that!

In the Harlequin novel, the night would be misty black with a howling wind and the moon suddenly covered by raging, turbulent clouds. In this reality, the night is simply dark, with a clear moon. I zip up my exposure, turn down the sheets and slip into bed. No reason to undress. No need to deny sleep.

♀

THE AD

Tori Joseph

*"Sybaritic GWF seeks flirtatious
femme fatale for amorous adventures"*

The ad was simple, direct, succinct, and inviting. It also haunted me for weeks. The rational part of me warned of the need for caution and practicality. The hedonist side advocated impulsiveness and indulgence. The struggle was annoying.

My dilemma was resolved one hot, hazy, humid Saturday in June. Maybe it was the warmth of the sun baking my naked skin to a golden brown that set my hormones on fire. Or, maybe it was just the possibility of introducing something new, different, and exciting into my mundane social life. Regardless of the motivation and ambivalence, I knew I had to respond to this unknown woman.

Her name was Arianna. Through the letters we exchanged, I learned she was a 38-year-old, well educated, well-to-do account executive for an advertising agency. Her letters reflected straightforwardness, intelligence, warmth, sensitivity and humor.

Most importantly though, she was very flirtatious and seductive. Each of her responses was written on a notecard showing women in increasingly provocative poses and decreasing amounts of clothing. Each stated a desire to meet. And, each described a romantic rendezvous we could experience.

I was obsessed. Arianna was increasingly intruding on my thoughts, stimulating an endless myriad of delicious fantasies just aching to be expressed. This was becoming the most exciting non-physical encounter I ever had with a total stranger. It was also the most unnerving. The intensity of my lust was frightening. With pen in hand, I began helplessly composing the letter that would take me to the point of no return.

Arianna,

I am attracted to you and your letters like a moth to a candle's flickering flame. Yet, I fear being scorched should my wings bring me too close. Nonetheless, my body yearns for your warmth so much that I am intoxicated and weakened by the fantasies.

The warmth emitted from your letters makes everything around me feel so cold and lonely that my body can't help but respond to you. I suspect you do it intentionally, allowing your words to slowly arouse and seduce me, embracing me tighter than your arms and legs ever could.

If I dared to stand before you, what would you do with me and to me? What would you do if I stood before you with my body and thoughts totally exposed and vulnerable? Would you seduce me further with your words, or would your mouth and tongue bring pleasure to my body in other ways?

I wonder if your lust and fantasies could ever match the intensity of mine. Tell me, Arianna, what would you do?

Tori

Her response arrived several days later.

Tori,

You are quite the tease, aren't you? Using your words to excite me, to provoke me, to entice me. You beckon me closer and closer to you with each and every letter, challenging me with your desire.

Yet my dear, it is your ambivalence which challenges me the most. I sense the hesitancy as you reach out to me. I feel the conflict when you tell me how I affect you.

Yes, Tori, I feel your fear, and it is that fear which excites me. that fear is what hardens my nipples. That fear is what produces the sweet nectar pooling between my legs. It is that fear which fuels the rapture you stir deep inside of me.

Your fear, my sweet, is not unfounded. When you choose to play with me, you choose to play with fire. I am the mistress of the flame. I can stoke it, inciting it to burn hotter and brighter than you can ever imagine. Or, I can make it linger, allowing it to dwindle until the glow is barely noticeable.

You sense the danger, even now, as you read the words in front of you, don't you Tori? You feel torn, a part of you wanting to flee, to run swiftly and steadily away from me as quickly as you can.

Yet, you are paralyzed, inexplicably drawn to me, anxious to know me, desiring of my touch. You are longing for my warmth, hungry for my passion. Your body aches for the ecstasy you know I can bring you.

You must decide, Tori. Will you choose to come play with me, to open yourself to me despite all the uncertainty, risk and danger? Or will you become trapped, a prisoner of your fear, choosing to let me walk out of your life forever?

I wonder which you will choose? I wonder how badly you want me? I wonder how much you are willing to risk?

I anxiously await your reply.

Arianna

My eyes and thoughts were glued to the words written on the card in front of me, reading and rereading them. I was stunned and speechless. I felt transparent. Never before had anyone perceived and stated my doubts and feelings so clearly. I did want to flee. But, try as I might, some inexplicable force was propelling me forward into the unknown.

Arianna,

I choose to play.

Tori

A week later, a dozen yellow sweetheart roses arrived. An engraved invitation accompanied them.

Meet me at the Copley Plaza
Saturday 8:00 p.m.
Suite 1206

Arianna

At 7:55 p.m. on Saturday, I stood outside Suite 1206 at the Copley. My heart was pounding. My breathing was shallow and quick. My rock-hard nipples strained against the fabric of my dress. My panties were wet with anticipation. Raising my hand to knock on the door, I paused briefly to recite the single lesbian's prayer, "please Goddess, just don't let her be a relative of Jeffrey Dalmer!"

Receiving no response, I turned the knob. The door opened easily. Slowly, I entered. Candlelight illuminated the room. Chopin's "Nocturnes" played softly in the background. I walked past the table set for two and the bottle of champagne chilling on ice, out the sliding glass doors to the balcony. I was settling my overstimulated hormones in the cool night air when I felt someone behind me.

Turning, I found myself staring at the most magnificent looking woman my eyes had ever seen. Arianna was tall and slim. She had long, flowing, dark hair, piercing, dark eyes, and a wickedly sexy smile. The short, white silk robe she wore was open to the navel, revealing a deep, even tan and ample breasts.

"Hello, Tori. I've been waiting for you," her soft and sultry voice said. "How are you?"

"To be honest with you Arianna, I can't help but feel like a fly about to become entangled in the spider's web."

"That's an interesting analogy," she chuckled.

"Is it an accurate one?"

Arianna poured two glasses of champagne and joined me on the balcony. "What if it is?" she asked, running her fingers along the top of my forearm.

"Then, I presume we will have a wonderful evening," I

answered readily as our fingertips met.

Arianna moved closer, pressing her body against mine. "In that case, it's nice to have you in my web," she whispered before placing her soft, sensuous lips on mine.

"It's nice to be had," I responded just before our wet, hot, hungry tongues found each other.

"It will be, darling, and I think making love would be the perfect way to begin our evening."

"Shall we begin right here on the balcony?" I asked, untying the belt on her robe.

"The first time should always be in private, my love," she answered. Taking my hand, she led me to the bedroom, and to one of the most erotic adventures of my life.

WOMAN IN THE WINDOW

Patricia Roth Schwartz

The heavy scent of the magnolias draws me out, out to walk the streets of this quiet, affluent, beautifully landscaped neighborhood, old with respectability, security, the authority of years in every brick wall, every lush tumble of ivy, every massive hundred-year-old tree. Lacking all of this in my own life – I want what I think these silent streets, these solid mullioned windows can give me. Magnolias in the north bloom for such a short space, the carnival-colored azaleas before them, the passionate lilacs following, I know I need to be out each night when I should be home with my note cards and rough drafts, or in the library checking and cross-checking references; a thesis seems irrelevant as the musk from the creamy blooms overwhelms me. I walk and I walk, and I need, of course, as always, to turn the corner by the majestic sycamore to see if, high up in the attic apartment of the house with the sweeping veranda on three sides, I can detect the light I always look for, if I can see, behind the lacy sweep of curtain, the woman in the window....

. . .

I think it's spring again. I'd like to crank the old casement shut if I didn't need the air, up here in the attic apartment, so badly. I don't want to smell the alluring fragrances of the season of life. Up here I've been able to escape all that. Yes, I have the plants: their roots are bound by pots, much as are mine by the walls of this snug space. A lucky low rent in such a district; the owners are friends of my deceased parents and want a respectable, quiet tenant. I turn out book after book, not the kind of stuff that would embarass them, but history, biography, always of obscure 19th century women, nothing smutty. They haven't figured out that I'm a lesbian, since I have no visitors.

I meet my few friends, when I do go out, at the cafe by the library in the bright light of day. Here, tonight, when I work best, by the window for the air, only for the air, no one is with me. I have no lovers. No one ever stumbles sleepily out my door in the early morning light, a dreamy grin on her face, her hair uncombed, her clothes obviously from the day before, carelessly put back on. I make love to the keys of the word processor. I live out the dusty passions of the long ago and the faraway, in the lives of those I write about. Tonight I have made great progress with my chapter. It s a bit chilly; I might even close the window so the scent of that magnolia can't draw me, can't stir the body through the faint cues of memory back to a time before, a time when I loved and trusted, when springtime meant the swelling of buds not only in nature but from the body of the lover, a time when trust was betrayed and love was extinguished like a candle flame in a gusty draft. It's ten past ten, the time she usually comes, the woman who walks these streets without fail, the woman who looks up, who, I know in my bones, although I would rather my bones forget such things, watches me. She does not see that I see. Tonight I will push back the filmy lace curtain just a bit, to watch her, my one small indulgence, as when I was a child I'd let one lozenge, fruit-flavored – my favorite was lime, or was it the cherry? – on my tongue, until its voluptous sweetness had finally melted totaUy away. Then it wiU be back to work, back to work till almost dawn. Then the day comes and I sleep til mid- afternoon. I rise, shower, trek to the library, the corner grocery, briskly, then back here again to safety. Yes, she's here again. I look. I stop looking. I get back to work.

. . .

I think the woman in the window might have spotted me looking up at her; a lamppost from the corner sheds a certain amount of light. I hope I haven't frightened or startled her. I suppose a man looking would create a different impression, a level of fear and dread. I don't want that, of course. I don't want her to notice me at all. I step back quickly into the shadow of the sycamore and linger longer than I have intended to. She's working, I believe, typing, it appears, but sometimes she stops and stares off into space, letting her fingers run through her long, wavy dark hair, as if that helps her concentrate. I wonder how soft it is; somehow I know its fragrance, with the soft scent of ferns in a woodland, the grace note of a rare, delicate flower rippling underneath. I imagine I am touching that hair, pulling it softly back from her pale throat, that I am kissing ever so gently that throat, feeling its sweetness, feeling the faint tremor of desire running through her body.... I must stop this; it has been far too long since there was anyone in my bed, my heart, my life. When you leave the one you once loved – no matter how much you needed to go, knowing there was no future, no deep meshing of two so different – it is a long road back to opening those closed doors once again.... I see the curtain pulled across. I force myself to walk on.

. . .

I awake with the merciless sun of midday melting the thin curtains, melting my eyelids, flowing molten and red over my flushed face and tangled limbs. The covers, rank with sweat, bind me. I kick them off and plunge into the shower. Full summer seems to have hit us, if only for a day. I was dreaming; my head feels thick with images, sensations, part of me stuck back in that dream scene, reluctant to leave for duty, routine, work. There was a woman in the dream.... I can feel her touch. Her kiss on my throat, her hand pulling my hair back off of my face, as others, especially one other, have done before, long ago. (Perhaps this is why I do not cut my hair, long after others my age wear sensible styles.) I grab the soap and the sponge and scrub. As my hands run over the surfaces of my own body, I feel compelled to let them linger, to caress, to touch, to raise to song melodies almost forgotten. I seem to remember that I have breasts, nipples, that tingle and throb, that become stiff and hungry, thighs with skin of unbearable silk that could loosen and open, secret places that could swell and ache and burst with juice. I can smell those damned magnolias again. I cannot shut the windows today – too hot, too hot. I am crying. I have been working too hard. I will go to the library and verify references, mindless scut work. I will return home, eat a simple salad, bathe again, and retire early. I will not sit up by the window tonight, the curtain pulled back, and watch and wait for her. I realize now it was her in the dream, the one who was touching me, the one who has been looking at me. Tonight there will be no light on. The window will be dark.

———————— ♀ ————————

. . .

I wonder if she's all right. The window was dark tonight, the light off, no shadows, yet all so real, figures just behind the tantalizing lace. I think about her now all the time. I'll walk by in the daytime to see if the mail is collected, the paper taken in, a nameplate still on the door. Maybe I could speak to the landlady – a concerned friend, haven't seen her for days, is she all right? I realize I don't know her name, the nameplate would only tell me her last name, even if there is one. I feel bereft, as if I have no purpose. I dreamt of her. I know it. She was bending over me, the dusky hair sweeping my body, the gentle swells of my belly, her fingers running easily over my limbs, circling in closer and closer to the curly tufts of hair that hide what it is I want her most especially to touch, the place I want to feel her hair sweeping, the place I want her fingers to search, parting hidden lips to seek out even more hidden secrets, releasing the notes of a song I had not even remembered my body could sing. I long to rest in the warmth and coziness I imagine her rooms to contain. I long as well to be part of the ordered work that seems to go on night after night within that shelter, since I myself can do no work. Has it all stopped now that the window is shrouded, its light extinguished?

. . .

I have heard from my publisher. I can afford this indulgence no longer. Tonight I am back, no matter what, by the window, working. I will not look out. I will imagine that I hear footsteps, but I will put that fantasy away just as I must all of the others of the woman on the walk approaching the steps, ringing the bell, bringing me armloads of magnolias which she heaps on the bed, just as she leads me, gently enough, yet with a certain urgency, to tumble with her amidst them, to find the blossoming of her body and mine, to release the fragrance that our own tightly closed petals hold as well. What draws me even more is the feeling I have for her of freedom, of being able to exist in her world, of how she can walk the night; the sweet breezes and scents do not endanger her. I long for her to be here with me, yet the fantasy carries me along further: after we have sated our appetites, after sweet sleep has claimed us, entwined together, we arise and go out into the

*world, she as my leader, my neat and ordered rows of books and notes
and drafts and galley proofs, left behind in their proper place. With her
at my side, we race down to the square where the light-spangled
fountain dances in the moonlight, past the strolling minstrels with
their tin cups at the curb, their beribboned intruments, their earnest
renditions of requests, their grins as ringing quarters hit the cups. I
imagine she would especially lead me to see the one I used to favor, the
man who could walk a tightrope he strung between two trees; juggling
flaming torches, he leapt off, always catching the torches in one hand
with an easy flourish, to give a sweeping bow. I want to live like that;
with her I believe I could....*

. . .

Thank the gods and goddesses she was back tonight,
although I hung in the shadows and did not betray my
presence. I am glad she' s not young.... There is a vitality about
the middle years I associate with her work and her purpose.
Her body is lithe, but not with the dieted slenderness of callow
youth. She is like me; I realize that now. We have our certain
thicknesses and slownesses, as much as we have the fineness
of lines about our eyes and mouths, faint silver veins on belly
and thigh, yet there is a marvelous beauty about her. I haven't
seen her face, really, only in my dreams and in my daytime
mind, but still I know it. I know from the tumble of plants in
her window, the little pots on the sill with the fuzzy-leaved,
jewel-toned African violets, and the cascade of the bridal veil in
the casement with its starspill of tiny blossoms, that she
treasures beauty and life. I imagine, though, that the world I
stalk each night is not hers, or has not been for a long time. I
long to bring her out into it. After our wanderings, we would
return to her world, to the crisp lavender-scented percale sheets
and plump goose-feathered pillows, to chocolate in little china
cups before bed (if we hadn't just fallen into sated slumber as
we lay, dripping with love), and breakfast, laughing, oranges,
croissant crumbs all over the sheets.... I imagine that I know
exactly how at the moment of climax she would cry out, how
she would taste – a ferny, musky, almost chocolate taste,
indescribable – how she would grasp my hands as I brought
her there, my mouth so close to the source of all life, as her

back would arch and her throat, and the song neither of has heard in so long would burst forth.... I realize that I am weeping, back here in the shadow of the tree. The magnolias are suffocating me. I must run.

. . .

This is dreadful. I sit here in the pose of the worker, the responsible meeter of deadlines – and all I can think about is her. From what I have seen from up here, she is no child, but along a bit in life, like me. She's not tall, she's sturdy; her hair looks bright and soft, sensible, but sensual, too. I imagine that her eyes dance. Her smile accompanies them. I go further than that; I almost feel the ripple of her cool silvery tongue against the swelling of my desire. My thighs ache to be parted, my secet passages ache to be entered. My breasts are as sore as my once-pregnant friends have told me theirs were before the birth. I want her. I want to open her up to me; I want her to open me.... I know she s out there, just beyond the shadow of that tree. Funny, I feel no fear, as I would if a man were stalking me out there, a potential marauder or intruder. Who I feel out there, instead, is my other half, my sister, my friend.... What would it take, flinging the casement wide, calling out –

. . .

I must linger in this place no longer. I must return home and resign myself to the life I have laid out – or I must make a bold gesture to claim my salvation.... What would it take, stepping out from the shadow, letting the light from the corner lamppost spill over me, the light from the window above beckon me on, calling out –

. . .

"Let's walk down my favorite street again."
"You mean by the big sycamore?"
"Yes."
"You mean the one where you always used to see the woman in the window? What an incurable romantic you are!"

"Yes, I know, but I love to believe that everyone is as happy as you and me. Knowing what our love has meant all these years, I guess I feel safer believing lots of other women can have it, too, that it's not such a rare commodity after all."

"How do you know she' s happy?"

"Because for so long she was alone up there – and then I began to see someone in there with her, another woman...."

"You goose! How do you know they're lovers?"

"I know."

"When you snuggle up to me like that I know what you have in mind when we get home!"

"Ummm-hmmm.... Oh, look – they're up there now. You can see the two of them just beyond the curtain, that lace one I like so much."

"Yes, I see them – I've noticed many more plants in the rooms up there – I've noticed, too, a garden planted in the side yard where there was only scruffy grass before, a kind of wild garden, all tumbling full of unusual things, wildflowers, even a few weeds that bloom – I don't see them in the window every night."

"Yes. Sometimes I imagine they go out to the square to the cafes, to hear the musicians, to meet many friends – look, they're inside now, though – they're moving close together. I think they could be embracing. They're pulling the curtain closed – they've put out the light."

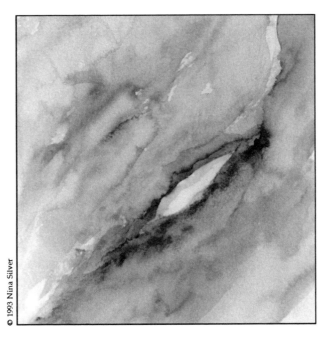

© 1993 Nina Silver

DOUBLE ASTRAL YONI

♀

IN FRONT OF EVERYBODY

Deborah Kay Ferrell

There she is, the prettiest child I ever gave birth to living in her Maw Maw's, my own precious Mama's house, with another woman. And she was the prettiest thing you ever did see, still is and it just breaks my heart. When she was borned she wasn't ugly and all red faced like all youngens. No m'am. Her skin was as pink and soft as a rosebud and she had a halo around her head the color of pure gold. And those eyes. Big and searching and always wanting to know. When she could barely walk she asked me, "Mama, who put my top on me," with her hand on those precious curls.

I grabbed my first child, feeling her sweet little body against mine and I said, "Why, Jesus did."

See, I raised her right. Taught her to fear the Lord. Dressed her up like a doll for Easter. You should see my pictures of her with her white lace bonnet and the yellow dress the color of lemons with petticoat after petticoat under it. She has her hand, which looks like my Aunt Helen Fay's, whose husband shot her, with her little pinky crooked like she's holding a tea cup.

Lord, Lord how I love that child and she has done gone and broken her mama's heart. It's that college to blame, I reckon. Before then, she was perfect and she won ever beauty contest she ever entered. Even old Libby Higgonbotham's girl, Verdie, was a senior in high school before she won that. I just can't understand.

You see it all started when she was at school. I'd call her up at 8:00 on Saturday morning and she'd get all snappy and I'd hear giggling on the phone. Now I knew Eva Marie lived by herself. She had to, nobody else could get along with her. And

I'd hear soft laughter and it didn't belong to no man. Then, Eva Marie would say, "Mama, can I call you back later? I'm busy," all hateful like.

Well, I'd like to know who in the world is busy at 8 o'clock in the morning. Anyway, I had that sick feeling in my bones like I did when Helen Fay said she was going out for a walk and she never came back. Then, they found her body on the jetties as cold as a preacher's thing. You know, that thing. Well, before she could hang up I asked,"Eva Marie, are you in bed with another woman?"

And she said, "Mama, don't be crazy."

But I knew. I knew.

So they up and moved to town. Eva Marie and that woman that I knew but didn't know about. Now the other one is smart, I'll grant you that. She works down at Jimmy Beckett's filling prescriptions and selling stamps. Don't ask me how the U.S. Postal Authorities gave Jimmy a permit to sell postage stamps. I think it must have something to do with being invited to Nixon's inaugural ball in '72. Anyway, there she is for the whole town to see and they look too. What's more, Eva Marie traipses in there every day with her lunch.

I'm telling you what. I almost had a heart attack and died when Bernice Divine, my next door neighbor, came over with a slice of her twelve egg pound cake and the town's latest gossip. Bernice said she was in there at twelve o'clock on the nose waiting to get her blood pressure medicine and in walks Eva Marie with a plate of food so hot you could smell it. Well, the other one just drops what she's doing and closes up the pharmacy and they walk out together like the whole world don't exist. When Eva Marie used to take Randy Ward his supper at the mill she'd wait and wait out in the car. Of course she couldn't cook then, so she'd buy it from the Winn Dixie deli and stick it on one of my good plates. Anyway, Randy never shut down the mill, not that he could have anyway, but he was always busy shoveling another log into the wood chipper so that he couldn't come traipsing out whenever he pleased. Well, let me tell you, Bernice was plenty mad when she had to come back at 1:30 to pick up her prescription. I was so sick I couldn't eat my pound cake and all I could do was look at Eva Marie's picture on the wall. It's the one where she's won Miss Mullette and she's standing between the man with best beard, Tommy Wayne, and Harvey LaCoss and his eight-pound prize-winning mullet. It was the biggest fish that was caught during the festival.

Anyway, Eva Marie has never told me, but I know. Hell, anybody with one grain of sense can tell. You should see the way they look at each other. Their faces and eyes go all soft and the love is plain enough for the whole world to see. That other one, I've got to give you that. She's got pretty eyes, prettier than my own Eva Marie's. They're the shape of huge almonds and they're the green of my own home state's valleys in the middle of the Spring. Why they're even greener than Scarlett O'Hara's in *Gone With the Wind* and they've got the longest black eyelashes you've ever seen. And no mascara, of course she wouldn't wear that. Anyway, the only time I've ever seen people look at each other like that is in the movies. Hell, neither one of my sorry husbands ever got that look on their face when they looked at me.

And you should see the way they take care of each other. When the other one so much as hints that she might be thirsty, Eva Marie up and runs and brings some iced tea with a lime wedge cut just so. Then, hell, it starts all over again. The other one says, "Thank you." And Eva Marie says, "You're welcome," and that look goes between them.

Eva Marie reminds me of Mama. That's the way she was. When Orville would holler, "Ruth, bring me something to drink," Mama would hop up faster than a jack rabbit. Of course I never did hear a thank you out of that man's mouth.

I can't figure it out. Eva Marie is pretty enough to get the best looking man around and so I go over to Maw Maw's, now Eva Marie's and that other one's house, and things are just so pretty. Why you should see Eva Marie's (and that other one's, you can't fool me) bedroom. I went over there one day and as usual I inspected the house and you should have seen the bedspread, and the dust ruffle and pillow shams with matching curtains and wooden shutters beneath them. And I said, "Well, Eva Marie, when did your pickle boat come in?"

And she said, "_____ " (the other one, I can't even bear to say her name) bought this for me. I saw it in the

Neiman Marcus catalog and the next week it came via United Parcel Service. Isn't that sweet?"

"Ooomph," I said thinking about Sodom and Gomorrah and how Eva Marie wouldn't even get a chance to turn into a pillar of salt. So, I sat down on the bedspread, it's dark green and peach, and you can tell it's stuffed with real down just by the way it feels and I looked at Eva Marie. Her face is more beautiful now, if you can believe that. It's peaceful just like the pictures of the Virgin Mary in the Catholic Church. Now mind you, I'm not Catholic but they hold a bazaar once a year and me and me and Bernice always go. So, I think back to when Eva Marie was dating Randy Ward and how she would sit in the living room without a light on and cry when she knew his shift was over and he wasn't coming to visit. Her face was thinner then, like a regular beauty queen's but there was something hard, almost starving about it too. I ain't seen that look on Eva Marie's face since I started calling her at 8:00 in the morning and she was too busy to talk.

Anyway, so real delicate like I say, "Eva Marie, what are you going to do with your roommate when you get married?"

Eva Marie just kind of laughed and said, "Mama, I'm happy just like this."

Well, of course I expected that, so I said, "Honey, but you're so pretty, you can get any man you want."

And then you're not going to believe this, but she said, "Mama, I don't want somebody to love me for the way I look. Beauty, after all, is a transient thing."

Well, you could have blown me over with a whisper. I didn't say anything more, but when I went home I pulled out the dictionary, the one I got for my high school graduation, and looked up that word: TRANSIENT: PASSING AWAY QUICKLY, NOT LASTING OR PERMANENT. Well, I thought about that one for awhile and it made no sense. Eva Marie knows that she won't even start losing her looks until she's fifty. Why, I'm forty-nine and all I've got is some very small crows' feet around my eyes. A little Oil of Olay is what does the trick.

So, I sat in the kitchen awhile and looked at the picture of Eva Marie with the bearded man and the mullet until it got dark and still I sat trying to figure it all out. Eva Marie isn't like me. Why, when I won Miss Great Smoky Mountains, I loved all the attention, and I've still got my crown. Not the dress, though. I had to borrow it from my old step-sister, Viola, who didn't even make the second cutting and that very night she demanded the damn thing back. Eva Marie, though, she didn't cry once when she was standing high up on that podium in the middle of the street with a sash wrapped around her and a dozen of roses in her hands. Then she came home and put her crown and her sash into a box and then she stuck it under the window seat. So, I'd pull out the crown and put it on top of the piano with mine and her sisters who were also Miss Mullettes and it would disappear. Finally, I gave up.

That's what I'm going to do now. Of course it's an embarrassment what with Bernice always running over here and telling me what's going on, but I've prayed and sent in seed faith money to Oral Roberts and got him to pray, and it just doesn't seem to be doing any good. Anyway, they're quiet and Eva Marie never sits alone in the dark crying anymore. Plus, her housekeeping skills have improved. Before the other one, she was as filthy as Sandra Ripley, and as I said before, things are just so over there now. Anyway, nobody ever ordered me anything out of Neiman Marcus.

THE MATURING OF MOOGHAN

Nina Silver

Mooghan didn't like her name. It would be bad enough had it only been that seldom-used relic, a "middle" name. But "Mooghan" came first – in fact, was the *only* name – on her birth certificate. She gave an extra hard push in the hammock that Roseann had slung for her between two redwoods. Even the shortened "Moog" that her peers and even Roseann had begun calling her, didn't help. She clamped her brow into a furrow that seemed too deep for fourteen years.

Not only did Mooghan have a weird name, she was adopted. The birthmother she never knew had left her all alone to deal with the consequence of her name. Lost in thought, the girl didn't notice how greenly the new summer sun was sifting its mellow light through the trees until a shadow fell across her eyes. "What's the matter, Mooglet?"

Mooghan wrinkled up her nose. She knew Roseann was only trying to be affectionate, but everything was making her feel touchy these days. She sounded slightly annoyed. "Nothing, Roseann."

Roseann sighed. "Honey, you can't mope around like that and then tell me 'Nothing.' What's the matter?" – although Roseann had a pretty good idea. This wasn't the first time they'd been through this. She waited, patient as usual.

"Roseann, when you adopted me, why didn't you change my name?"

Roseann leaned against one of the trees, caressing the girl's flame-colored head. Her own hair had been that color when she was younger, she recollected. "Moog. We don't know who your birthmother was, or anything about her. But if she called you 'Mooghan,' she must have had a good reason. It's too unusual a name for someone to just pick out of a hat. I'm sure it must mean something. Your name is the only thing that connects you to her. So when I adopted you, I thought it very important that you keep the one link you have to your mother. I still feel that way."

She continued to stroke Mooghan's head until the child relaxed. Then Mooghan's voice cracked. "Roseann, why would someone go to the trouble of giving me a perfectly hideous name, and then – leave me?"

Roseann took Mooghan in her arms. The girl half-heartedly returned the hug, and this time Roseann stifled her sigh. "Sweetie, the moment I saw you I loved you. That's never changed. And I know your birthmother loved you too. But sometimes a woman can't keep her baby, no matter how much she'd like to. I'm sure your mom was very upset that she had to give you up."

Mooghan frowned again: she still wasn't convinced. She got up and wandered listlessly in the direction of the house, leaving Roseann to her own thoughts. Had she done the right thing? In not changing Mooghan's name; in choosing to raise the girl herself; in allowing Mooghan to call her "Roseann" because she insisted on it from the time she could talk, even before Roseann told her she was adopted. And what about Roseann's most recent decision, their move to the northern California mountains where the closest neighbor lived six miles away and the nearest town was a thirty minute drive? The spacious, low-beamed house that Roseann had worked so hard to acquire was nestled on forty acres of land, with a huge pond for Mooghan to swim in and trees for her to climb. It was beautiful in the woods, but was the price of living here too high? Mooghan had still not settled into her new school. Moody and aloof, she seemed to be having more trouble than usual making friends.

But even if Mooghan had them, Roseann contemplated remorsefully, how could she go visiting when Roseann couldn't spare the time to drive her to those places that were out of the range of Mooghan's bicycle? She labored long hours at her job, often on weekends, and came home late. The last project she and Mooghan had completed together was the treehouse, and that was two summers ago when they'd first moved to the mountains.

As Roseann walked toward the house with an uncharacteristically heavy step, she stopped as she saw Mooghan at the dog run. The girl was with the stray she'd found last week, a feverish, starved mutt whom no one, not even the regional vet, thought would make it – no one, that is, except Mooghan. She spent the next seven days and nights feeding the dog a homemade remedy out of a dropper bottle and massaging her to get her temperature down. When Roseann urged Mooghan to get more sleep, the girl refused, saying simply, "Ethiopia's going to live because she knows I'm rooting for her."

Today, the dog looked like a different animal. Mooghan looked brighter, too, as she gently brushed her coat, murmuring "That's okay, Ethiopia, I won't hurt you, that's a good girl." Mooghan had nine dogs now, all with exotic-sounding names like Starfire and Jellybottom. If she had to be stuck with an unusual name, Mooghan had explained to Roseann, she might as well spread it around.

Roseann waved and smiled, and Mooghan waved back. Then the older woman glanced at her watch. "Moog, I have to go to work," she called. "I'll be back tonight around seven-thirty. Supper's in the fridge. Don't wait for me if you get hungry."

"It's okay, Roseann, take your time. I had breakfast today. We can eat dinner together."

What a plucky soul, Roseann reflected, as the car rumbled along the driveway that snaked out to the main road. *Mooghan certainly is different, though it's much more than just her name. There is something almost uncanny about that child. She's one in a million. Then again,* Roseann acknowledged with a chuckle, *so am I. We make our choices in life and live with the consequences as best we can.* The sun glinted into the seemingly bottomless pond, casting a still, dark image of the nearby firs. The old vacant manor bordering the opposite side glimmered back, as tightly shut as it had been since the day they moved there.

School let out, summer plodded into July, and Ethiopia became plump. One evening, when the sun poured its last gold into the indigo sky, a station wagon followed by a huge van rolled up to the house across the water. A man, woman and girl piled out of the car, workers opened the van, and soon they were all bringing in boxes and furniture and lamps. Mooghan, who was outside with several of the dogs, watched the proceedings in amazement. The house was no longer empty! Flashlight in hand, she raced across the open field with Ethiopia barking close behind; and late that night when Roseann came home she heard all about Mooghan's new friend. Claire was super nice, and not only did she have a mother and father, Mooghan prattled away, she had the tiniest hands you ever saw and could scale trees like a squirrel.

Roseann, elated and relieved herself that Mooghan finally had a playmate, welcomed Claire with open arms. The two girls quickly became inseparable. Claire, having lived in a town her whole life, insisted on exploring every acre of woods and going on "adventures." She and Mooghan hiked and swam, hung out in the treehouse, played with the dogs, and placed bets on whether Ethiopia was merely filling out or had become pregnant. Claire was sure it was Mooghan's constant attention and feeding that had caused Ethiopia's weight gain, but Mooghan swore the dog was older than she looked. I can't watch her *all* the time," she explained, proudly patting the dog's belly. Claire was shrewdly philosophical about losing the bet: "If she's just gaining weight, I win five bucks, but if she's pregnant and I lose the bet, I'll still get a puppy."

Mooghan's new neighbor fascinated her. Claire was everything Mooghan was not: springy and quick and dark. Though a year older than Mooghan, Claire was small – her hands, height, even her nose. When she was alone, Mooghan would undress and inspect her pale freckled body in the mirror, marvelling at how gawky and angular she seemed compared to Claire's swelling curves. At night in bed, Mooghan touched her chest that had just begun awakening to plump new buds, and thought of Claire already ripened, full and round. She often fell asleep like this.

One unusually scorching day, Mooghan campaigned for Claire to go skinnydipping with her. Claire balked. "No-o," she faltered, "I don't want to."

"Why not?"

"We-ell...it just doesn't seem like something you're supposed to do."

This didn't make any sense. It also didn't sound at all like

Claire. Mooghan, mystified by her friend's reluctance, decided to try persuasion. "You like being in water wearing material that's clingy and uncomfortable the moment you get wet?"

Claire remained silent, so Mooghan continued. "It's stupid to swim with your clothes on. You only undress anyway to take a bath. Why can I be naked when I'm in bathtub water, but not in swim water?"

Claire, no longer hesitant, removed her shirt and shorts at lightning speed and raced into the water. Mooghan followed more slowly and got undressed too – after noting with surprise that Claire had not been wearing underpants. No wonder she seemed reluctant to take off her clothes! Mooghan watched intently as Claire submerged her entire body for a moment in the crystalline water, searching the sandy bottom for heaven knows what. Lucky for her, Claire couldn't see her staring.

"Claire." Mooghan scrambled after her, shivering a little – probably from the bracing temperature, she thought. "How come you don't wear undies?"

Claire couldn't hear. She'd dunked her head in again to admire some fish and when she came up she was choking on water. Mooghan pounded her on the back so hard she almost knocked Claire down.

"Are you okay?"

Claire nodded.

"So how come you don't wear undies?"

Claire, obviously embarrassed, blinked her mahogany eyes. "Because. You don't know everything about me, you know."

Mooghan gave her wet hair a toss. "Well, there are things about *me* that *you* don't know." Deliberately, she waited.

Claire took the bait. "Like what?"

Now it was her turn, Mooghan thought, to act superior. "I'm not telling."

"That's not fair!"

"Sure it's fair."

"No it's not." Claire emerged from the pond and stood on its sloping pebbled bank so she seemed taller than she was. Mooghan couldn't help noticing the little brush of hair that was darkening the tawny skin between Claire's legs. "Come on, Moog, I did something I've never done before. Now it's your turn. You have to tell me your secret."

your turn. You have to tell me your secret."

"Okay, but not here. Let's dry off and go to the treehouse."

Soon they were settled in their private fortress, sharing a cream soda that Mooghan had stolen from behind the paper goods in the pantry. This was part of Roseann's private stash, tucked away because she didn't want to encourage Mooghan's habit of eating sweets between meals. Obviously, her efforts at hiding the forbidden snacks hadn't been too successful.

"I'm ready." Claire, her dark eyes huge, looked at Mooghan expectantly.

Mooghan soberly contemplated those eyes. Why was she so unnerved when she gazed into them? She leaned luxuriously against the wall, her rust-colored curls straggling across her face. Acting more aggravated than she felt, she brushed them aside.

Claire was becoming impatient. She finished off the cream soda with great slurps until she was satisfied that every drop was gone.

"All right," Mooghan finally said, as if preparing to announce the entry of a mystery guest. "I'm going to tell you why my name is Mooghan."

Claire stared. Mooghan took a deep breath; it was too late to stop.

"I am named," she declared, "after my great-great-great-great-grandmother, who was Queen of Scotland."

Claire's eyes got even bigger.

"She and the king were inordinately rich. But they were also very kind. During the winter she would bring the poor into the palace kitchens and feed them. Everyone loved her."

A smile flitted across Mooghan's lips as she closed her eyes, imagining the scene. "I take after her. She was very fair, with the lustrous blue eyes and reddish gold hair that people from those parts are known for. My great-great-great-grandmother was a very noble woman," she proceeded with relish. Mooghan was enjoying herself greatly.

"Wait a minute," Claire chimed in. "I thought you said great-great-great-*great*-grandmother."

"I did," Mooghan snapped, annoyed at being interrupted. "I said 'great-great-great-great...grandmother.'"

time. The second time, you said 'great-great-*great*-grandmother.'"

"That's what I said," Mooghan retorted. "Great-great...." She stopped, confused. In her enthusiasm she had forgotten to count.

"I don't believe you," Claire returned crossly, her eyes narrowing into slits. "Really, Moog-han, I think you're making this up." She half rose, as though she were getting ready to leave. Without thinking, Mooghan touched her arm.

"Sit down," she commanded, trying to keep the panic out of her voice. "It's no big deal."

"Why should I stay? You lied to me." Claire looked at Mooghan in such a way that it sent a pang straight through Mooghan's heart. "Why?"

"Why what?"

"Why did you lie to me?"

Mooghan squirmed and bit her lip. "Because."

"Because why?"

"Because," she blurted out, "I hate my name and thought that if I told you something wonderful about it, I'd be special." Too late, an uninvited tear dropped into Mooghan's lap. Claire regarded her gravely.

"Moog, don't you know I like you? Why would you need to make something up?"

By now Mooghan had slumped into a corner, sobbing. She hated crying in front of people almost as much as she hated her name. "I'm – I'm adopted."

Claire was silent for several moments. "Moog, I didn't know! But you don't have to feel ashamed. There's nothing wrong with being adopted." Mooghan's sobs grew louder. "Moog, it's all right." Alarmed, Claire sat close and patted her friend's knee. "I don't think your name's funny. It's special, different – just like you. I mean that in a good way."

Mooghan lifted up a bright red face, sniffling. Furiously searching her pockets, she remembered that she'd left her hanky on the kitchen counter when she'd gone into the house for the cream soda. In case Roseann could detect fingerprints, Mooghan had opened the pantry door with her handkerchief. You could never be too careful.

Quickly Claire assessed the situation. In a twinkling she had

Quickly Claire assessed the situation. In a twinkling she had her shirt off. The label read, 100% cotton. "Here, use this."

Mooghan hesitated. "Go ahead, it's soft, like your hanky." Claire brought the shirt right up to Mooghan's nose. "Don't you want to get rid of your snot?"

The girls laughed. Encouraged, Mooghan blew loudly. But she couldn't stop shaking. Between noseblows, Mooghan's eyes kept falling on her friend's breasts.

Circles of dark pink protruded upward, surrounded by soft mounds. At least, they looked as though they'd be soft. Mooghan's fingers started to itch. Not knowing what else to do, she rubbed her eyes.

Misunderstanding, Claire grabbed Mooghan's hands. "Listen, it doesn't matter to me where you came from."

Mooghan gagged. "Really?"

Claire squeezed her hands tighter. "Really. I love you. I'd love you even if you came from elephants." She said this so solemnly they had to laugh. But in the ensuing silence that dominated each breath, Claire's declaration reverberated through Mooghan like a wave. *I love you....* It made her feel tingly and cold all over, nervous and wonderful at the same time.

They stayed like that for what seemed like forever.

Finally Mooghan spoke. Her voice was hoarse. "Did you mean what you just said, about – " she couldn't bring herself to utter it, so she tried another word – "about me being...special?" Dammit, she fumed, why was she having so much trouble getting this out?

Claire didn't seem to notice. "Of course I did, Moogie." Mooghan was startled. Claire had never called her that before, but she kind of liked it. "Moogie, why would you think I didn't mean what I said?"

There was no way Mooghan could answer. In vain, she tried to stretch her legs, which refused to budge. Suddenly there wasn't enough room in that cramped little space.

Claire let go of Mooghan's hands so she could grasp her friend's shoulders. "I always mean what I say. I'd never lie to you, Moogie."

Mooghan shuddered. Claire gripped her tighter. "What's the matter? Are you all right?"

squeak.

"Moogie, *are you all right?*"

Trapped, Mooghan stared at the other girl. "I like you too, Claire."

Claire nodded.

"A lot."

Claire was still holding on to Mooghan's shoulders. She gave no sign of moving.

"I mean...a *lot lot*." Mooghan's hand somehow found its way to the back of Claire's head. Their faces were so close that Mooghan could feel her friend's breath. It was warm and steady and rapid.

She gulped. "Claire...."

Claire gazed at her intently. The nipples on her bare chest stood erect, like proud pines.

Their lips found each other easily.

Time was a suspended twilight of tongues and lips. There wasn't much clothing for Claire to remove. Mooghan's was off in a twinkling. Skin met skin, hungry. Enjoying a boldness that belongs only to youth, Claire and Mooghan made their first love in the treehouse with the earnest ache of souls who never question the folly of being vulnerable, knowing only how good it can feel. Mooghan's eager mouth explored Claire's nipples, twirling them round her tongue while Claire clung to her, trusting. Claire rubbed and fondled the sensitive little bump between Mooghan's legs with her fingers until Mooghan could stand it no longer and bit into the shirt that was clean. They embraced wildly, moaning, stroking each other in moist moving rhythm until their shivering insides exploded. The energy between them streamed and penetrated and gushed so they could not tell where it began or ended....

Two hours later, the girls were still in the treehouse. Only when the sky darkened did they reluctantly part.

The summer was enchanted. Mooghan smiled more and started humming songs to the dogs, taking extra special care of Ethiopia who, at this point, was indisputably expecting a litter. When Mooghan wasn't having dinner at Claire's, she always waited up for Roseann so the two of them could eat together.

One night Roseann didn't arrive home until ten. Mooghan was sitting at the kitchen table, sullen and forlorn.

"Oh Moog, you shouldn't have waited for me."

Mooghan's voice was husky. "I always wait for you now, Roseann." She studied the floor.

"You're right, Mooglet. I should have called." Roseann opened the oven door and pulled out the dish that Mooghan had been keeping warm. Its contents were bone dry. "Do you mind a little crust on your casserole?"

Mooghan shrugged. "I'm not hungry."

Roseann tenderly touched her cheek. "Moog, I'm really sorry. I had no idea you'd be waiting up for me this late. Part of the delay was a stop I made in the opposite direction from home to pick something up for you. Do you want to see it before we eat?"

Over dinner, Mooghan kept stroking the two embroidered velvet cushions that Roseann had brought for her. "What's that smell?"

"Isn't it nice? They're filled with cedar flakes. I thought they would be perfect for the treehouse."

Mooghan nodded excitedly. "Claire'll love these."

Roseann studied the girl's face carefully. "You're spending a lot of time together, aren't you?" Mooghan flushed. "I think that's lovely, Moog," Roseann said quickly. "Claire's a terrific girl."

Mooghan looked enormously relieved. "Did you know Claire's father has been teaching her how to debate? He says the world's become a bloody mess since he was a boy, and no daughter of his is going to be caught unprepared. He figures Claire should have as much right to mouth off as anyone else." Mooghan laughed. "Isn't that neat? And her mom...Roseann? Roseann, what's wrong?"

Roseann didn't answer. Her eyes had mistily unreeled to a past she had not thought of in years. She was older than Mooghan, but in some ways not quite as stubborn, not as reckless. Or was it a matter of courage? She sighed. She wished someone had given her two plush pillows....

Mooghan's trebly concern transported her into the present. "Roseann?"

The woman looked at her, a little sadly. "Yes, Mooghan. I'm all right."

"*Roseann*! Call me *Moog*, okay?"

Early next morning, Roseann packed some sandwiches and drove down the mountain – not to work, for she had decided to take the day off, but to the main library of the nearest major city two hours away. After pouring through stacks of dusty, thick volumes, she got back in the car and drove home, a satisfied smile on her lips.

Roseann didn't see Mooghan after that for three days. An emergency had come up at work, and she needed to make up the lost time. When she returned home nights, Mooghan was sleeping.

On the third evening, when the overdue moon struggled to push its way through a thick spread of clouds, Mooghan spied the flash of a lantern in the treehouse. With a pounding heart, knowing it could only be Claire, she glanced at the empty driveway, pulled on her jeans and a shirt, grabbed a flashlight, and darted out the front door.

Claire was lying on one of the sweet-smelling pillows, munching popcorn.

"Claire! What are you, nuts?"

"Not nuts, popcorn. Try some – it's a party." Gleefully, Claire threw a fistful into the air. Popcorn flew in all directions.

"Claire, you're crazy. How on earth did you slip out? Won't you get into trouble?"

Claire scrutinized her with mock hurt. "Me? In trouble? Moogie, you wound me. What makes you think I didn't ask?"

"You mean your parents let you come out here?"

"Not exactly. I told them I'd been invited to sleep over at your house. I just made a little detour here first, because you didn't yet know that you'd invited me. I simply had to see you tonight." There was a wistfulness to her voice. "I missed you."

Their kiss lingered, sweet and electrifying. Soon both shirts were off. They did not undress completely – it got chilly in the mountains at night, even during the summer; and Claire, in the excitement of her plan, had not thought to provide them with a blanket.

But even the bite in the air finally began to dissipate. Mooghan had unzipped the fly to Claire's jeans and was fingering her wetness. They lay in a leggy sprawl, panting and groaning with each impassioned caress.

Abruptly Mooghan spoke. "Claire, we'll never tell anyone, will we? This is our secret."

Claire froze, then propped herself up to look at Mooghan. It was hard to see, though; the light from the lantern was flickering out. "I don't know why it has to be a secret. Aren't you my best friend in the whole world?"

Mooghan flinched at the unmistakable reproach in Claire's voice. "Yes, of course you're my best friend – in the whole world," she added hastily, realizing how hurt Claire had sounded. "But what we're doing is..." She drew in a breath.

Now Claire sounded testy. "Why does this have to be a secret?"

"I don't know, it just doesn't seem like something you're supposed to do."

Claire thought for a moment. "Moogie, that's what I said to you the first time we went skinnydipping together."

Mooghan giggled. The truth of her own wisdom had circled back to her.

The beam of a flashlight zigzagged through the trees, and they heard the low crackling of twigs being walked on.

"Moog!" The girls recognized Roseann's voice. "Are you there?"

"Quick," Mooghan hissed, "get dressed!" Trembling, they pulled on their clothes in a flurry of motion. If Roseann noticed later that they were wearing each other's shirts, she said nothing about it.

"Moog! Is that you?" It didn't occur to Mooghan until later that Roseann easily could have probed a treehouse window with her flashlight. "You'd better answer her," Claire whispered.

"Yes, Roseann, it's me," Mooghan's voice faltered through the dark. "Uh...Claire's here."

Roseann's unruffled tones lilted through the branches. "How nice." She was now at the bottom of the ladder, pointing her flashlight on the ground. "It's nippy out. Wouldn't you girls rather be at home in a warm bed?" Mooghan was shivering, but Claire doubted that it was from the cold. Somewhat unsteadily, they clambered down.

Immediately the moon broke through the clouds, casting down an eery glow. Roseann looked hard at Mooghan as if to convey something, but all she said was, "Honey, next time leave me a note." Then to Claire: "Why don't you come back with us and stay with Moog tonight? We'll phone your parents if they don't already know where you are."

Enormously relieved, Mooghan grabbed Claire's hand without thinking. Roseann spoke before they could separate.

"I'm so glad you moved here, Claire. I think Moog was a little lonely before you came." She reached out with both arms. Mooghan hesitated, her lower lip quivering, then rushed forward, tightly clutching Roseann at the waist. Roseann held her close.

"You know, Moog – Moog*han*," Roseann said, carefully. "Your name really suits you. I haven't had a chance to tell you, but I found out the other day that in the British Isles, centuries ago, the people worshipped the Goddess Morrigan. She was so greatly loved and revered that her sacred shrines were under the guardianship of queens." Roseann paused. "She was also called Mugain." Wide-eyed, as though jolted by an invisible ghost, Mooghan gave a sudden little jump and exchanged glances with Claire.

Roseann continued in her calm way. "'I hold secrets that will liberate you. Come, discover who you are,' Mugain would sing. She had the power to cause enormous transformation in those around her – just as you've done with me. I can't imagine life without you."

Even beneath the silvery cast of a swelling moon, Roseann and Claire couldn't see Mooghan blushing. But it would have been all right if they had, she realized, holding Roseann even tighter. With Mooghan in the middle, the three of them walked arm-in-arm back to the low-beamed house in the redwoods by the edge of the pond.

FLASHBACK

Karen Latimer

When the doorbell rang, Zena Rae McCloud, Houston's mom, set aside her copy of *Ladies Home Journal* with the interview of former First Lady Mamie Eisenhower and told herself she would finish it after supper.

She got up to answer the doorbell on her way out to pick strawberries for shortcake after dinner. Her huge garden stretched along one side of the yard from the back of the house to the old barn, which was unused except as a place to store garden tools, ice skates, and an antique Model T her husband, Garrison, had inherited from his grandfather along with the house and a few acres.

Zena Rae was from Texas but Garrison's folks had been in Ohio since John Chapman, known as Johnny Appleseed to some, had preceded and then become friends with the first settlers. Ohio was the Wild West back then.

The only thing that bothered Garrison about his family tree were the rumors about Appleseed and Raphael Patrick McCloud, a fellow Swedenborgian, who willed his property to his brother's only child when he died, because he'd never married and had children himself.

Garrison was a country lawyer who, after all these years, was still madly in love with Zena Rae who was as gorgeous as the day he married her. A lot of people thought she looked like Esther Williams, the movie star in all those aqua musicals.

The doorbell rang a second time. Zena Rae opened the door and gave her fourteen year old daughter's best friend, Stacey, a "Hi!" and a big hug. "Go on upstairs, honey."

Then from the bottom of the stairs she called up, "Houston – Stacey's here!"

"Come on in," Houston said without looking up. Chin in the palm of her hand, elbow in her pillow, diagonally sprawled across the top of her mostly blue bedspread, Houston was nearly all the way through *The Agony and the Ecstasy*, Irving Stone's soulful biography of Michelangelo.

"Wow. You're almost to the end," said Stacey, noticing that it was an awfully big book.

"I'm going to be an artist when I grow up. You would absolutely not believe how cool Michelangelo is." Houston put a pressed leaf bookmark in the book, closed it, rolled over and sat up. "It's a good thing you came at the end of a chapter because I might not have been able to stop."

"You're always like that with books. Me too. I should find out if there's a Book Addicts Anonymous for us." Stacey went to Alateen sometimes. Her mother was a lot better, now that she'd been going to AA for over a year.

"Yeah – do you think we could make a teen book club out of it?" Houston thought a gathering of book addicts would be great.

They laughed. Neither one would have willingly been divested of her favorite pastime.

Stacey plopped a package that looked suspiciously like it had a book inside it down on the corner of Houston's bed.

"When you're finished with that one," Stacey said, as Houston extricated the book from its pumpkin-colored construction paper wrapping, "you're going to love this one."

"Gosh, Stacey, thanks," Houston glanced at the front and back covers and dust jacket flaps, done in non-sensational Catholic printing house style.

"It's to maybe sort of help make up for inflicting my catechism class stuff on you," Stacey offered. "Believe it or not, there are some neat things in here that you'll like."

"St. Francis of Assisi? Even though you know I like biographies, I'm pretty sure Michelangelo is about as close as I can get to religious stuff now – cause he was that kind of artist, they all were then. I still have that ragged fingernails feeling from you telling me more than I wanted to know about original sin, which, by the way, my mother said the Presbyterian version is about the same as your version."

"Not my version." Stacey wasn't willing to embrace it either.

"Ragged fingernails is about right. It's not fair to all the little kids since then."

Houston's and Stacey's theological innocence had been traumatized and transformed into theological angst.

"Are you still a pantheist?" Stacey had been impressed with Houston's ability to find a suitable alternate religion when it didn't seem like there were any in Magnetic Springs, Ohio in 1963.

"Yes, but I also include angels," Houston replied. She wasn't sure early nature worshippers included them, but she wasn't going to leave them out. She liked the notion of having friends out there in the universe.

"Well good then, because you're gonna like this St. Francis book." Stacey reached up and readjusted the green rubberband on her pony tail.

"Gee, Stace, it's a hardcover and everything. Of course I'll read it. Isn't he famous for being kind of a wild saint?"

"In more ways than one," Stacey's voice took on a hushed, conspiratorial tone. "First I saw my mom reading it and she said he was a rowdy, eyes-for-the-girls, lush before he got sober and started fixing up an old fallen down church practically with his bare hands because he heard a voice."

"You mean he started out a regular guy?" Houston was interested.

"Yeah. He was a rich merchant's son and the cutest guy in town. Even after he got holy, everybody always liked him, because he was fun." Stacey sat down on the top of Houston's desk.

"Really? Didn't he get seriously bummed out about original sin?" Houston was still somewhat dubious.

"Maybe they weren't pushing it right then," Stacey offered hopefully.

Houston turned the book over in her hands, and noticing a turned down page corner, raised her eyebrows quizzically.

Stacey then rushed a statement she'd been holding for a surprise into the cradle of air between them: "He could fly – I mean, he floated above the treetops, and they saw him, a bunch of times. Later on in his life, that's what he liked to do."

Houston leafed through the book looking for drawings of him doing just that, but there weren't any.

"It's in there. No pictures, but there's old records of eyewitness accounts which the author put in. They sell it right in Our Lady of the Rosary bookstore but they never tell you *that* part! My mom says St. Francis was a yogi. I looked it up in the encyclopedia and he had a lot of those same powers, like in India."

"Wow. This is better than anything we learn in school." Houston did like school and got all As and Bs, but her inquiring mind ranged further into studies of her own, biographies of neat people and things like Druids and artists and Mayan pyramids.

"I know you're not so hot on Christian stuff right now, but St. Francis is neat and even the animals liked to talk to him so he must have been easy to talk to. Wolves even. And he could fly. I mean he floated. I know you'll like that part a lot."

"As soon as I finish Michelangelo. It sounds great!"

With that Houston gave Stacey a hug and wondered, for a half a moment, if she would ever work up the courage to give her best friend a real kiss. Like in the movies.

Maybe the next time one of them stayed overnight at the other's house. Maybe next Saturday night after the hay ride.

. . .

The hay ride was pretty cool – brisk air, sunset, laughter, horses, a hay fight that ended up with hay in everyone's hair and down everyone's shirt, started by a couple of rowdy boys hoping to cop a feel in the general melee.

The girls were great but the boys were, as usual, immature; maybe there would be hope for them someday. At least that's what Houston and Stacey thought, though some of the other girls had mad crushes on a few of the more decent boys, the ones who seemed likely to join the football team or become doctors in the far future.

Stacey and Houston were two of the cutest girls in school but they thought it was more important that people be good conversationalists. They liked people who read books and the newspaper and thought about deep things. And laughed a lot, that was important too. They speculated about Edna St. Vincent Millay and her bohemian friends in New York in the twenties and wondered how they would find people like that when they finally escaped from Ohio which was awfully pretty but not too exciting.

After the hay ride they had cider and doughnuts, then the kids parted company around 9:00 p.m., except for the ones who lived right in town who went to the coffee shop. Jill's mother came and picked up all the kids who lived off the highway north of town in a big station wagon and dropped Stacey and Houston off at Stacey's house along the way.

They made hot chocolate and let the marshmallows melt in it while they built a fire in the fireplace. They put a Patsy Cline album on the stereo and moved other records towards the front of the pile, including Johnny Mathis and Edith Piaf, the French singer who made them feel so sophisticated whenever they listened to her. Stacey's mom and dad had some great records.

Stacey's family was in Cleveland for the weekend, visiting her grandparents and going to the museum and the Cleveland Symphony Orchestra. Stacey's mom, knowing Stacey cared more about the hay ride, suggested Houston stay over for the weekend. Stacey thought about bubble baths more than hay rides that week.

She had been kissed by two boys so far, but it had done nothing for her, it was awkward and minus any excitement. She knew who she wanted to kiss. Houston. Her best friend.

Houston had been kissed by one boy who she didn't care if she ever kissed again. It was Katherine Hepburn movies that stirred her heart, and Edna St. Vincent Millay, and Stacey.

After they talked about the hay ride and finished eating soup and cheese and crackers in front of the fire, Stacey suggested bubble baths because they obviously had to do something to get the hay out of their hair and stop scratching.

Houston thought a shower made more sense or there would be a lot of hay floating around the tub. But she wasn't opposed to the idea of a bubble bath afterward, since Stacey seemed to have this bubble bath idea.

They flipped a coin to see who would get to shower first. Stacey won and jumped in, then called Houston to come in and join her. Houston thought that sounded pretty exotic, but fun.

She'd never taken a shower with anybody before, just two people alone. Under the hot water streaming down their lithe bodies, they soaped each other up and hugged a slippery hug that felt better than either of them had ever imagined a hug could feel and looked at each other like they had just been the first people in the whole world to invent taking a shower together. They stood and swayed under the hot water, kissing, first one tentative kiss, then one kiss going into the next. Since Stacey had invited her into the shower and washed her back first, Houston had turned around and kissed her, something she had wanted to do for a while but had not imagined quite like this.

After their shower, they decided to take a bubble bath anyway. Together. This was no ordinary night. They didn't know exactly what was going to happen, but it was happening.

Even if they only had what was happening, whatever it was, a couple times a year when their parents were out of town, it would be worth it.

Lounging at separate ends of the tub, with second cups of hot chocolate and marshmallows perched on the TV tray table they set up next to the bathtub, Houston looked at Stacey and said, "If there's such a thing as past lives, and there must be or I wouldn't feel thousands of years old at such a young age, do you think we were ever together before?"

"Yes, I think so," Stacey said. "We're best friends now, but I think we were in love before, like maybe a lot of times. Or maybe we were just real spiritually close, like friends in a monastery."

"We're not in a monastery this time, at least not yet." Houston wiggled her slippery, wet toes under Stacey's arm and tickled her.

Stacey laughed and jumped up, splashing a little bit of water on the floor.

"I'm waterlogged," she declared.

"Me too," said Houston, getting out.

Stacey didn't just hand Houston a towel, she patted her dry, with flourishes she had picked up from the romance novel she had just read that had a bubble bath scene in it. Fiction could facilitate real life if it gave you a good idea, even if you had to translate a boy/girl thing to a girl/girl thing, not hard to do if you loved your friend and courage and imagination struck you simultaneously, like a meteorite that might hit you both if you were standing together in the same place out under the stars.

Stacey stood up after leaning down to pat Houston's legs dry. Stacey was still wet, the bubble bath water evaporating slowly from her skin. She wasn't cold yet because she been in hot bath water for so long.

Houston kissed her again. Like in the movies. It seemed like the only thing to do.

And it seemed the most natural thing in the world because they really loved each other. As friends, but there was something more to it and they didn't think anything could or would ever shake their friendship, so they followed their first kisses, and turned over the Edith Piaf record, and soon they were rolling over and over and over, tumbling through the universe together on a blanket in front of the fire, swooping feather fingers and feather kisses everywhere.

Beneath young breasts just recently announced and young nipples that seemed to have a life of their own, and other places responsive to kisses that came naturally if one were going from head to toe, they felt shooting stars ricocheting with pleasure from point of light to point of light, sky maps of light within and between them, oceans of light with waves to ride, very wet waves, inside, warm as the tropics.

Much, much later, after the fire in the fireplace died down, they went up to Stacey's room and pushed the twin beds together and fell asleep in one another's arms.

Kisses in the morning, and newly discovered sex again, with solemn I love yous. And they laughed, with joy and funny cosmic observations, and they worried together a bit, and talked about that.

Then after breakfast, they watched "Meet the Press" on TV because they both wanted to help save the world someday and wanted to be well-informed citizens. They thought they should part company before Stacey's family got back, and get busy with homework and chores and other things, because they didn't want to seem too dreamy.

But, it being such a beautiful sunny day, first a glorious bike ride down country roads to find a place in the woods where they would be able to kiss again even when both their parents were in town.

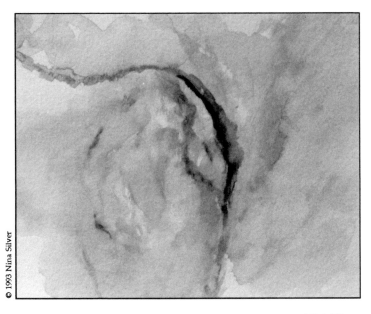

© 1993 Nina Silver

SPACE — TIME CONTINUUM YONI

CARE IN THE HOLDING

Maureen Brady

LAURA waited nervously while the woman filled out the contract for the rental car. "Two seater okay?" she asked.

"Sure," Laura replied, confused about the question which barely touched down in her float of mind. What was she renting – a motorcycle? Minutes later, she found herself checking out the two-seater – indeed a car – a sporty Ford with bucket seats up front and a long hatch in back. Placing her directions on the other seat, she headed for the Bay Bridge, for her rendezvous with Chana, whom she was picking up at cousin Richard's in Berkeley Hills. Her mind printed an image of Chana – brown eyes with a sparkle in them, soft cheeks, sweet smell – and her heart sent a streak of excitement straight down her gut and into her loins. She'd be lucky if she made the right turns, so excited to distraction was she. She'd been sitting on this excitement a whole month now, since the hike they'd taken back east, which had tripped off a great glow in her heart.

She pulled off the road and stopped in the hills when she sensed she was nearly there, and tried to gather herself. Prepare. For what? She knew it would be good. She knew they liked each other. She knew the day on the mountain had been like magic and they were the same two women coming together again. Breathe, she said to herself. She took ten long, deep breaths. On the tenth, she realized she hadn't even checked to see if the charge was correct before signing the contract for the car rental. She dug it out and looked and got further confused because they hadn't filled in the charges. But, of course: they were waiting to see if she'd return it on time. More deep breaths. She felt light-headed, maybe hyperventilation. What will she be like? The streak of adrenalin in her gut again. The feel of energy in her center, intense, like if she wasn't going to move that car, her clitoris would be willing to drive. Go on. Jump. The waiting has been long enough already.

She started up the car. The next left was the cousin's street and time speeded up. She was at the door ringing the doorbell. The door was large, opened out. Disorienting. She'd pictured Chana receiving her, inward, with the opening of a door, but now this door. What?

Chana pushed it open, came out herself with the door and gently hugged Laura, who was near to fainting. Chana radiant, wearing red, eyes friendly; her short dark hair started down over her forehead, then curled back. She invited Laura in. Laura smiled yes, speechless, don't ask me to talk. Chana took her to the back porch where cousin Richard and girlfriend were sitting. They showed off a hummingbird, and the flutter of the hummingbird's wings felt like the stir inside her chest. The house was built on the side of a hill, and the porch felt as if it was suspended in air. She glanced at Chana, caught the intensity of her beauty, and felt as if the house was going to slide down the cliff. Said to herself: keep breathing. Said to them: "Exciting to live here. You must feel on the edge all the time."

"I don't notice it at all," said cousin Richard, oblivious to the intensity of her feelings.

Chana took Laura on a tour of the house. In the bathroom, she kissed her. Laura held Chana's head, held their cheeks pressed together and, heart pounding, began to feel recognition from the last time. She felt the ways they were strangers acutely, and wanted to hold their bodies together until they knew all the connections that were there.

"Let's say goodbye and go," Chana said.

Her cousin wrote out a series of turns to the Richmond Bridge. Chana seemed composed, able to follow the directions, while glancing at Laura, flirting with the sparkle in her eyes. Laura went closer to the edge of the porch, looked out over the long view, but still couldn't look down.

They left. They got lost on the first turn but drove on somewhat aimlessly.

"What's your take?" Laura asked Chana.

"I think this will get us there."

"I like the way you follow your instincts," Laura said, going on down through Berkeley, feeling both cocky and lost. They were getting to know each other the same way. Laura alternated between having faith in that instinctual plane and feeling a stranger, both to herself and to Chana. What if they were going blocks and blocks in the wrong direction? She wanted to be at the ocean, out of the car. She wanted to be where they could hold each other. Yet she was glad to have the mission of driving. Needed time to establish a sense of Chana in the real flesh, not fantasy, before they made love. For the past month, they had written sweet and tender love letters; encouraging words, sharing of fragments of their lives such as food tastes, favorite books, excitement about the work each was doing at the moment. Laura had been in residence at a West Coast artists' retreat, while Chana had been home in New York preparing to turn over her first book to her publisher.

From the moment she'd arrived in her place of retreat, Laura had noticed that the bedroom alcove was more fit for romance than for thinking up stories. The king-sized bed was made enchanting by the two walls of windows which wrapped around it. Outside, the branches of an oak reached in close to the windows, and the patterns of the leaves, black at night, had a dreamy feeling to them. In the moonlight they lost their distinct edges and became blots placed in some mysterious order. They offered an entirely different impression, green, in the mornings. She had loved sleeping there, dropping into the dream reality of night, then waking into a gentle California green. She awoke with a kind of relaxed openness she hadn't experienced for a long time. And it was in that openness she yearned to wake and look upon Chana's sleeping face next to her. She wanted that openness, that wonder she had seen in Chana's eyes as they pulled back from kissing up on the mountain and looked each other full in the face.

They had found and crossed the Richmond Bridge and were headed for the coast when they came into a misty fog. This was Laura's first time seeing it like this. The other times she'd driven up Route One she'd seen that magnificent long view of the rugged shoreline from the headlands. Now the fog closed around them, and even when she knew they were near the ocean, she couldn't make it out. She'd only imagined bringing Chana here to the long view. Taking her by the hand and leading her down to a quiet spot on the hill and watching her take it in. The view as awesome as the strong feeling that traveled breast to breast as they held each other. Now what? Chana took her hand and kissed it softly, then held it to her own heart. Laura smiled, warm inside. Scared, too. Who was Chana? Who was she? Why were they feeling so much while knowing so little about each other? She darted looks at Chana but the curving road required her attention. Next time she saw a place to pull off, she did. Said let's go down the hill a little and see if we can hear the ocean.

They both got out. Laura stretched, releasing some of the tension. It took a second for her to realize she was standing still, it was the car that was moving. Rolling backwards. She ran for the door and hit the brake. Embarrassed at her driving ineptitude, she turned red. "You're distracted," Chana said, coming around. Laura put the car in park and pulled hard on the emergency brake, then laughed.

"The navigator will have to see that the car is not left in neutral."

Chana pulled her out and hugged her and kissed her. "Lucky we weren't on a big hill," she said.

They moved down to a point where they could see the waves crashing in on the rocks below. First they sat huddled close, as they had on the mountain, and kissed, smelled each other's hair, felt the deep magnitude pulling between them. Then they lay down. The fog created a room for them. They couldn't see the road or the sky. Sometimes they could see the ocean, sometimes not, but always they could hear its rhythm. They held each other and rocked together.

"How I've longed for this," Laura whispered.

"I know. I know," Chana replied.

Their lust flushed their faces as they lay side by side, the full length of their bodies pressed close. The fog provided privacy. The room it made for them was impersonal, without decoration. It had no square corners, no flat walls. It moved in close. A gentle kiss grew into deep passion. When they looked again, the fog had thinned and the room expanded.

Laura felt one with her body and with the cliff they lay on. Her hand moved slowly up and down, charting the soft contours of Chana's body, remembering the curve of her back from the last time. She followed the line of Chana's firm thigh and pictured the gracefulness with which she must run.

Chana pressed her pelvis closer and Laura's lust peaked in response, sending charges like lightning, sharp through her body and back to Chana. She was breathless, delirious, joyous. Chana murmured how she loved her smell, rolled on her back, and Laura rolled with her so she was on top. Laura pressed into her, tasted and smelled Chana's neck, and inhaled deeply of the moist ocean air. She felt the hummingbird stir in her chest while her cunt both beamed a radiant heat and received the hot waves of Chana's sexual energy. Suddenly she wanted her naked. She wanted to be inside her, feeling the moisture she knew was there, wanted to have her own self known that way, free of the covering and constriction of clothes, but she knew this, just as it was, a kind of bliss, deserved its full due. Like a rose opening to full bloom, beautiful in all its stages, it had a timing of its own. She arched her head back and saw in Chana's face a desire that matched hers. How expressive that face was, how its movement reminded her of the waves below. Desire charging, cresting, then ebbing back as her closed lips fell into a quiet smile, broadening her face. Time was no more distinct than the boundaries of the room – seemed long if Laura thought of how much she was alive for each one of these minutes, short in the sense that there was no more waiting. The waiting was over.

. . .

They stopped in a small beach town for coffee before going on to Laura's studio. Chana did most of the talking. Laura had trouble taking in the words or being verbal herself, though she wanted to make herself known this way. She had the precipice feeling again, like she'd had on Richard's porch, just from sitting across the table from Chana. She found her beauty so striking she was surprised the other people in the coffee shop were acting as if it were an ordinary day and not noticing this clear-eyed, extraordinary woman sitting across from her, sipping coffee and radiating joy. She went to the restroom and confirmed in the mirror that, sure enough, it *was* possible to see the radiance that *she* was exuding, as well. Her eyes looked greener, her hair looked a shiny, light brown. Her skin looked soft and clear, ruddy and inviting. The warmth in her pulsed so she felt brought close to her own essence.

. . .

When they arrived at the studio, she felt this closeness still, but also the strangeness of the place, hers but not hers, a gift for the month, and the strangeness of their knowing nothing of each other's homes. She led Chana around, pointing out the skylight dome at the peak of the building, the deck, the small kitchen, the charming bath. Still holding her hand, she led her down the two steps into the bedroom alcove. She fell onto the bed and leaned back, gazing out on her familiar and favorite view.

"Come." She reached toward Chana, who stood smiling, then came down next to her.

"It is paradise," she said, her voice almost husky. "You weren't making that up."

"Especially now with you here, it is," Laura said.

Then they held each other and Laura's breath went away. She gasped for it somewhere under the lust. She felt the firmness of her own body as well as Chana's as they held tight. It was dusk and the light played on Chana's face which was wonderfully variable. Sometimes soft with pleasure, sometimes scared, or suffused with passion – all looks welcomed by Laura as they broached the complexity of her own feelings. If she and Chana truly were strangers, why did their bodies seem already so well acquainted? And more than acquainted, as if they'd been waiting and yearning a long time for this meeting. They kissed deeply. Laura rolled on top. Chana put her hand at the base of Laura's spine and rocked her back and forth in a gentle rhythm, and Laura felt the sweet warmth growing in her cunt. She ran her fingers through Chana's hair, held her lovely head, and loved the rhythm they both followed then. Chana pulled their shirts up enough so their bare bellies touched and the warmth spread more fully to there. Laura felt their belly skins kissing – soft coverings overlying those guts pitched high with risk. She rose to take her top off and pulled Chana's off as well. Then they lay breast to breast and felt that warmth course through their chests. Laura cupped one of Chana's breasts in her hand and nuzzled down and tongued the nipple and watched it come erect. When she leaned back to look at Chana's face, Chana admired her breasts, saying they were perfect. Laura murmured her response. They rolled so that Chana was on top. Chana built on the same gentle but spunky rhythm. They built but did not come. What Laura needed for orgasm was no greater intensity than what they had already created; it was the building of trust. To feel the care behind Chana's caresses. And to trust that care.

Laura was raw in places, thin-skinned in her healing from the break up with her lover of many years. It had been four months since she'd left their home, their bed, many more since they'd been really alive, sexually, with each other. She remembered times when they'd put great effort into making love and she'd stayed for a long time on the brink, almost coming off that edge but not quite, not quite able to. She remembered after her father died, when she came back home from the funeral, how she felt so alone. Bess didn't seem to really be there. She was, but she wasn't. Laura didn't seem able to ask her for what she needed. More holding. More care. More care in the holding. Bess was still depressed herself from having lost her job, and Bess came from a family where death passed in silence, feelings held in. So Laura had gotten on this brink and stayed there, knowing if she came, it would be with a burst of tears, that her pleasure was enfolded by her grief. Sharing the pleasure when she was not able to get the care seemed a betrayal of her body. And her body, often truer to her than her mind, balked. "It's okay," she'd told Bess. "We don't have to be so goal-oriented." But Bess became reluctant to initiate sex with her, and this at a time when she wanted Bess to do the reaching.

Chana, on top of her, was close to her own size. Bess had been a good deal heavier and, with her, this position had verged on feeling stifling to Laura. She felt a wave of freedom at having made this choice, and the wave brought her back to the glow in her belly, in her loins. At the same time, she felt tears very close to her pleasure. Chana was rocking her again.

Comforting. The rhythm was right for her. How did Chana know to make it that way? Laura looked at her again to take in her face. Sweet, soft, mystery. She also has memory, she thought. Of what? Of whom? Where did this bonding, this movement towards intimacy, take her? Her concentration was strong, she was all there, deeply inside her body. She called Laura's name. She said, you, you, and Laura was awakened further by the call.

They stopped to kick off their pants and then coming together again was like another new meeting. Like when the door opened out and Chana came with it. Like when they first lay on the cliff and held their bodies full length. Their bellies and breasts, their lips and cheeks came back together, familiar, still new but knowledgeable, warmed to each other. Laura put her thigh between Chana's and felt the softness of the skin that pressed her own. She felt the moisture of Chana's cunt and the beam of heat that burned out from her. She held still because the feeling inside her was already so full and she just wanted to feel it. A deep satisfaction with the awakening of all her senses, her cells. She breathed in the sweet odor of Chana's neck, squeezed her own thighs and felt the heat coming out of herself. She reached to feel Chana's cunt. So nicely risen, soft and full like bread with good yeast. Her finger slipped on the wetness as she explored. She felt both nervous and exhilarated, like nearing the peak the first time she climbed a new mountain. Would she be lost? Would she be found? Hearing Chana's response, she knew when her touch was right. She slid into Chana's vagina, a close cave, warm and moist and soft as velvet. A home. A mystery. How perfect that vagina felt and how forceful its being. Like the tide they'd felt while lying in the fog. She wanted to look, and did. Pulled away from Chana and ran her fingers up the path between the lips of her vulva and saw how pink she was. "A beautiful pink garden," she murmured. Her own excitement increased with her words. She had rarely before expressed herself this way. It was a way of being active, of putting the feelings outside, between them, instead of tucked up close to her heart in a bundle the other would have to slowly work to penetrate. A garden was a place to grow in, a place of wonder. These caresses were the seeding of a love which might grow between them.

Chana pulled her back to a long body embrace, breast to breast. She held Laura tight around the hips and Laura felt the energy build heat in her belly. She felt the waves of Chana's energy driving her own higher. She felt her heart so full of feeling. This woman was a stranger, yet she knew her. T h e whole month following their hike back in the East, she'd felt Chana's presence very close beside her. A loving presence like a guardian angel. She'd felt her spirit in that very bed, and ached with wanting to have her physical presence there.

Chana, on top, raised herself up. She was radiant. Her eyes were joyous. Laura ran her fingers through her dark hair, which stood up from her head. Chana kissed Laura's breasts, her belly, as she moved down to Laura's cunt. There she became the explorer, parting Laura's lips and searching the area gently with her fingers, then licking her. Kissing her. Sucking softly. Laura kept her hands in Chana's soft hair to anchor herself as she rocked her pelvis. She felt vulnerable with the absence of Chana's chest against her own, with the open air embracing her there instead, but she could feel love in Chana's mouth on her if she allowed herself to feel there between her legs. It was hard for her to allow full attention concentrated on herself when she was not in the process of actively giving. But she talked to herself: *Take it. Let her love you. Let her find her own pleasure in this. Trust.* The receiving required more trust for her than the giving. But when she was able to take in the giving, she glowed inside and moved her pelvis in a way that welcomed Chana's loving. She felt very full. She was on the verge of orgasm. She was on the verge of tears. What would it mean to cry in this woman's arms the first time they'd ever made love? She did not come. She did not cry. Chana came back to hold her full length, her lips next to Laura's ear. Spoke in her soft voice, "I want you to come."

Laura's lust peaked at this spoken desire. "I'm moved by the way you touch me, the way you kiss me," she said, knowing as she released these words that they would take her past the tears.

"You can feel that . . . and still come," Chana said with quiet assurance.

"What about you?" Laura asked.

"I'm easy," Chana replied.

Laura felt the jets of adrenalin shooting from her heart to her belly. She felt her desire growing deeper, like a powerful undertow. Growing stronger and hotter as Chana's invitation ran in her mind. She reached down between them and spread both their lips so her clitoris pressed directly into Chana's, and moved against it. Chana whispered sweet words in her ear. Sometimes she couldn't make them out, but she could feel the care in them, the concentration. This was Laura and Chana together. Their histories were in them, all of the love makings of the past, but this now *was them*. Laura whispered Chana's name. She let her mind go. She was her body. She was the fire and the spirit that moved inside her. She rode it. She had been a long time waiting. Then she tripped off the edge and gasped and felt the glow spread inside her, like a sun coming out strong from behind a cloud. She moaned her pleasure. She felt the tenderness of Chana's arms around her. Her breath came quieter as she lay with her gratitude for the way this was possible, for the miracle of this woman, Chana.

Chana proved her ease. She moved with a confident connection to her body. She built, then stopped still for a moment, savoring some place she had reached that she did not want to pass. Then she moved again. She was calling Laura's name, she was speaking to her cunt. Laura looked at her face – so full, so fine with desire, it fired her. Then Chana's breath turned to cries, each breath was a cry, each cry had an echo. Each echo touched Laura's heart. She held her. She held her. She was so happy to be holding her.

TOP OF THE MORNING –
A LOVE SONG, A VOW

Donna Allegra

Morning. It's good to awaken and lie still. You hug close to the breast of dreams – my angel: safe under sleep's wing.

I need to pee, but I won't move and risk waking you. I want the moment to stay as it is. I can watch you freely, with no one to see how greedy the look in my eyes, how tender; that I'd gladly fetch whatever you ask and lay it at your feet, an eager puppy, my tail a wagging.

. . .

We slept, chilly but content, under a star-spattered sky. Almost 10:00, the sun melts the cold edge from night. I like our days on this women's land. As performers, we are royalty at the music festival. With the countryside as our fairground, we engage in the activities of daily life with one another – gathering food for meals made and eaten together, travelling to places and taking adjacent seats, each asking the other if she wants more tea, if she's ready to leave, squatting in the grass to pee.

. . .

In the late afternoon, sitting back to back at the edge of the lake, you'd told me, "The water will always support you." Never much of a swimmer, I've feared trusting water. Clear welcome reflects in the day, but I've seen the surface forbid and turned closed to color at night. You say that indeed evil forces exist in the world and that we must respect their power. You encourage me to accept the water in all Her aspects because otherwise we drown; but that if we stand by our borders, She will teach us well. Some games are not made for victory, so rather than go under, destroyed in a pointless struggle, we learn best by observing. The way of standing aside allows for a vision which is better watched than judged too soon.

I think you are a daughter of Yemanja, ocean Mother, sister of the fishes. From you I learn to go with whatever comes up and presents itself, to let myself be led: to trust. You said, "She will always support you" and I'm now baptized to a belief in the water. Long before the moon brought a face to reflect on the still surface, we rose to leave. We had been sitting back-to-back by the water's side and I wanted your sun-warm flesh to continue leaning and trusting my strength. But I know you'll hold to me later and I will always support you.

. . .

I feel a huge spirit breezing the trees. It's in the green leaves with the wind calling after, the way I'd reach out if your calm beauty passed by – a scent I can almost taste, form just outside my reach, a birdsong somewhere nearby. Desire fires me at the root, a slow syrup sapping through my core. It peaks through the crown like leaves overflowing their branches as if to praise the sky. This secret I carry through my days is your love. How to tell the others what it is to play guitar and have the instrument I hold dear be tuned by your voice? I touch the strings to reach chords and melodies I know by heart and fingers to find I've become your song. I appear to accompany you, but you pluck the sweetest notes from me.

. . .

Soft rain fell in the evening when the applause faded. After all these months, I still feel just like everyone else: awed when you sing. It's as if you've gone to the roots of language, biology, physics - all the sciences and arts of knowledge, and having perceived the flaws in our system, built the whole thing anew on a better foundation. Some part of us could comprehend everything you said, but no words were adequate to translate what you'd brought to life. You struck us blind by your vision and gave new sight in its place. We simply understood with that part of us which has a spark magnificent, and then, all we could do was cry because the ways we had to work with were mostly wrong and didn't help our blind eyes to see. We'd have to go all the way back to our beginnings to even try to get to the places you rouse. But hearing you touched memories of something good and true.

. . .

I feel like a very small child with you sometimes: a girl eager for her mother's smile, a word of attention, a touch affectionate. Thoughts toward you are lights burning out all the dark corners in me. I steal secret pleasure watching your body – neat and compact in the white carpenter jeans you wore last night. I considered the white bra lacing your cleavage under the East Indian shirt. The most beautiful breasts I've ever cupped and held dear are worn by you.

. . .

I like how you take space from me, yes, even that. Your need came first and after the initial sting of separation, I'm glad to be alone. I think on the pleasures of our conversations. We have taken things slow, in small strokes that way remains good to me still. It keeps unsung melodies from going underground and then surfacing blindly. I can trust and depend on you, though desire that we go the long distance is my anxious inner refrain.

. . .

You give me your all, open, brave and unafraid. We both carry an urgency to nest together. Our love takes shape as a flower that seeks the sun, becomes a youngster eager to grow tall and fly high. I find treasures precious with you – gifts I cannot make valuable alone. You let me care and become the vessel where I pour all my concern and protectiveness.

The other face of my joy is your hands reaching out to me. We share a feeling where one looks out for the other, where I let you help and you let me be tender, where we can each be butch and femme for the other. I'm not always the stronger, the dominant one in our situation, and some say I'm supposed to be. But I don't stand by those lines anymore. My truth sings that it doesn't matter that I wear pants, you wear make-up; that I'm taller, you have longer lashes; that I work with a wrench, you use nail polish. I was glad that first time you asked me to dance. I couldn't reach the brave energy to go to you. What a relief not to have to come from behind masks or shields or any kind of weaponry because I fear I'm not cute or butch or sexy enough.

. . .

I think back to yesterday afternoon. The sun nestled on my crotch where I wanted to cradle your head. My eyes took in the waves swelling from the waters they were a part of. I saw reflected in the great lake the sky covering everything, white clouds barely visible. How I'd like to contain and watch over you day and night. I have a sun, sea and sky of desires for you who touch the best parts of the world in me - the way waves rise up from the water, swelling to a point on the surface, then expand back down again.

We spoke about becoming mated lovers. I asked what you wanted, and looking me straight in the eyes, you said, "Everything – your caring and strength, the life of the spirit, all that I can have. I want a lot and believe I'll get a lot because that's what I'm willing to give. My fight is for the long haul. I'll work to stay a long time."

Yes, I want to be with you as a life partner. As I watch the miracle of you stir in sleep, fresh gratitude sears through me – not trembling hunger about to spill like a beggar, but soaring joy for the open palm. I'm no one so special that I deserve your love and know full well it's a gift given freely. My fullness was ready for yours. I drank deep and then could see how we're often blessed and surprised with so much more beyond the stingy portion that should be our just desserts.

Last night, after the applause and the backstage giddiness had settled, I felt proud to be with you – proud, like: this is my lady. Proud, like: I'm strong and will do battle to protect her –

you're the one I'd go to war for. Proud, like: possessive, though I wouldn't tie you down or try force on you, but proud, like: you're a part of me – mine because I know beyond doubt you want to be and I belong just as hard and fast because you are my choice above all else: I felt proud.

. . .

At twilight, we took our sleeping bags from the cabins to this clear space away from the others. The party looked good, but we didn't want to be there. A haze muted the sky's blue sheen as if a giant bird's wings had smeared wisps of cotton all around. You watched the birds sailing atop the setting sun – a last look before she rises from the water. I looked to the range of trees standing ever still and upright, the leaves leaned and swayed against each other as the wind breathed through them.

I saw in that moment the whole drama of life – not the theater of pain, the stage of complaints and the recital of sorrow. I knew everything important then, and now my desire is for nothing more than to stay and live with you by the water, curtained by the trees with the open sky to cover us. I could spend our time in this peace, off the fast track where doing too much gives back too little. I would have us sift our natures together, as wind in trees, the sky painted on the water, sun drowning twilight before dipping down to sea. My sight settles here where lives stillness as the important movement. All I know is in this morning where my love rises and folds her wings to rest beside you, my quiet center soon to awaken.

CARRYING COALS TO NEW CASTLE

Cody Yeager

Three A.M. The semester's papers are stacked in a neat pile on my desk, next to an illuminated globe. I like to sit here in the darkness, surrounded by books and maps, watching the world glow and listening to Smetana's river wind through Prague. I have promised not to write her any more letters; they upset her, you see. She doesn't want to know that nothing makes sense now, that the world blurs when I spin it too fast when I've had too much Scotch. She doesn't want to hear that the symphonic poem is only noise. So I don't write the letters and the words pile up inside in sloppy stacks. Hundreds of letters have already been sent; more would be like pouring a handful of sand onto the beach or dumping a pitcher of water into the sea. So, at least for tonight, I won't write.

I don't come from a long line of desperate people, if that's what you're thinking. No one in my family's history would sit until 3:00 in the morning, in pain, staring at the world through a drunken haze – all for someone who doesn't even speak to you? No. No one else in my family would be in this situation.

Knowing this increases the failure. They are not like me, rushing to the ocean to add sand and water. They are all far away and don't dream of my life; I never tell them. I know they don't want to hear it. We seldom speak on the phone, but I hear all their voices now, staring at my glowing planet. My mother's cuckoo clock hangs in my study and it chirps now, just once for the half hour. When we couldn't sleep, my brothers and sisters and I used to lie very still trying to guess the exact second the cuckoo would sing. His song was our surest lullaby.

Each night, my mother would tuck us in, always saying the

same thing: "G'nacht, schlaf gut." She never kissed us; she didn't see the point. Then, back downstairs, she'd go to Tolstoi and Hardy, the men she adored. We could hear her if we were quiet. The pages would turn and Beethoven would play softly all night long until my father came home from work in the morning. When piles of snow slid off the roof with a dull thud, we'd wake up and hear my mother humming symphonies. Outside our window, the night sky was not dark; it glowed red-orange from the mill where my father was. We imagined he was sending us messages when the molten steel was poured and the sky lit up. And then we'd listen to my mother's voice again and slip back into dreams.

My mother read her dreams because she could not live them. She could not. She had all of us; her time was spent teaching us to read, trying to make us eat with forks, buying school uniforms, matching wool kneesocks, explaining the ablative case in Latin, spending a fortune on food, and being the woman my father adored. He did, too. No matter what. He complained about the bills from the butcher shop, the bakery, the delicatessen, and all the rest. "Why can't you just shop at the A&P?" My mother never glanced up, just replied in her measured voice: "My children are not going to eat garbage."

And the bills were paid. On time. Out of my father's account, not hers. He would fill in the amount and sign his name carefully, pressing very hard. My mother would write in the name of the company getting the check. Her handwriting was like the examples on the flashcards at school, absolutely perfect. Since they both wrote the checks anyway, you might wonder why they didn't just share the account. My father wondered too. "What's a matter-you don't trust me?" Cool teutonic stare. Those eyes were never still, always darting here and there, surveying everything, frowning over some thick book. Nothing missed her glance: a puppy under the bed, a book and flashlight smuggled under the covers, a bottle of beer in my brother's bookbag for school. My mother had a long talk with my brother about the beer; school was the one element of our lives she was inflexible about. We would have an education whether we wanted it or not.

The nuns at school were from an old Polish order, they spoke with a strange accent - who didn't then - and they snapped rulers across our knuckles nearly every day. Steel rulers with a sharp edge. Each time I instinctively reached for a pencil with my left hand, that ruler would flash. Shame ran down my face in streams, but I never told my mother. She so much wanted at least one good student. And some of it came easily to me: grammar, Latin exercises morning and afternoon, reading, and geography and history. But not math; that was her downfall too. Sometimes, I would kneel at my desk for the whole hour while question after question was demanded. I never said a word; ashamed of my ignorance. And always the ruler.

My little sister told our mother everything that happened at school. Really, she didn't know when to quit. Like the time she was sent to confession for wanting to take her little dog to heaven, too. My classroom was across the hall and I could hear Sister Mary Georgine's voice bellow: "Blasphemy! Jesus, Mary, and Joseph! Blasphemy!" So my little sister went tearfully to confession, then blurted the whole story out as soon as we arrived at home. She was such a cute kid; she really didn't want to go to heaven without her dog, said it wouldn't be heaven. My father laughed it off, but my mother was very quiet and her face took on that this-is-not-the-end-of-the-dis-cussion look.

I knew what that look meant. See, the sisters were afraid of my mother; they didn't understand her, so they mistrusted her. Her dignified reserve meant one thing to them: cold distance. They were probably jealous of what a knockout she was; every grown up lady seemed to be. But you don't really think of nuns that way, I guess. Anyway, they could never get over the fact that my parents had different names. A lot of people couldn't get over it, I never understood why. "Unverzagt." It sounded so fantastic when my mother said her name – and so horrid when everyone else did. But she would never, ever have traded such a name: a name that meant (and sounded) fearless, undaunted, undismayed. If a name ever fit anyone, my mother's name fit her.

The very next morning, from my desk in the back of the class, I saw my sister leave the room next door and head for the office. We had just begun the Magnificat: My soul doth magnify the Lord. Feet flat on the floor, desk in perfect order, my hand shot up. "Please Sister, permission to go to the lavatory."

Normally, we all went to the lavatory at the same time, twice a day, and no more. But since I had done particularly well at translating Caesar's Gallic Wars that morning, Sister nodded approval. It was like that with nuns; you never knew what kind of mood they were in until it was too late. Anyway, I slipped down the hall to the office just in time to see my little sister come out, as white as the Holy Shroud of Turin. She held a finger to her lips as we passed each other. I could hear Mother Superior's voice shouting up a storm. And from time to time, the quiet, determined voice whose tone never changed.

The next day, an announcement was made over the loudspeaker. Since God had, in fact, created everything on Earth, it would not be improbable to assume that very special pets might be found in a very special section of heaven. That evening, my mother served us a Schwarzw – lder Kirschtorte and asked my brother to deliver one to the convent. He returned with a nice note: "Thank you for the Viennese Cocoa Cake." "VIENNESE!" They never got another cake; my mother is not one to make the same mistake twice. My father laughed it off, saying German, Austrian, all the same. Cool teutonic stare.

When she packed our lunches, my mother always put in extra fruit. Not for us, she knew we traded away our fruit for "good stuff." The extra oranges or bananas from DiGirolamo's Fruit Market were for the kids two houses down. Mike Gregorovich's children. Now that you ask, I can't even remember exactly how many there were. When his wife came over one morning in tears to tell my mother it was true, she was pregnant again, my mother just sighed. When Daddy heard about it, he said "Mikhail Gregorovich and more kids: if that ain't just like carrying coals to New Castle. He don't want the ones he's got."

Mrs. Gregorovich was Romanian and very religious. Mike was from Russia; my mother said he was a drunken communist bastard. Daddy said he was okay, just too easily carried away. "By vodka and a blowing skirt," was my mother's cynical reply. About six months after Mrs. Gregorovich's announcement, there was a pounding on our door one night. We had been just about to head upstairs in our footy pajamas, but now we waited to see who could be at the door.

Mike. Drunk as a skunk and in a mean mood, too. He had little Petey by the ear; he was always dragging one of his kids that way, as if they wouldn't walk without being forced. "This is only of my sons belong to me – Petrov. My slut wife is Craiovan whore dog. You, beautiful lady, will give to me many beautiful children. We leave now." Then he stood back and looked at my mother like she was supposed to do something about all this. And she did too. Still as a statue, she hissed "Schwein!" and slammed the door. Then she did something I have never seen her do before or since, something I myself would never dare do: she called my father at work. In fifteen minutes, we heard Daddy and some other men in the kitchen downstairs. Loud, angry voices. And now and then, that calm level tone. Then they left, looking for Mike.

The next day, my father came home with a present for my mother. Nothing new there; he was always bringing her the roses she loved, or chocolates, or something, anything, to get her attention. But this time was different. This time the present was a German Shepherd. A big German Shepherd.

My mother and the dog were inseparable right from the start. "His name can only be Wolfgang; it has to be." And it was. He kept a watchful eye over us because my mother commanded him to, but you could tell he was only half interested. He growled slightly when my father came home from work, creeping a little closer to my mother's feet. "Stupido," Daddy would mutter under his breath. But Mike never came to our door again.

In fact, I almost forgot about him, until I saw him at the butcher shop a few weeks later. He hurried out of the shop, never even saying hello to my mother. Always before, he would buy me a Clark bar and admire my mother's hair or her dress. Today he rushed outside. He had a hard time carrying his packages with his left arm in a cast and sling, his leg dragging behind him. Steep cement steps led up to their house; I guess they could be dangerous, especially after a winter's night of vodka.

It was shortly after that, if I'm remembering all this right, that Mrs. Gregorovich went into labor. She was in the hospital for two weeks and the baby was finally born – as dead as the stone lion at the children's zoo. Daddy said it was all that carrying coals to New Castle. My mother said it was the devil himself in the shape of a no good Russian. Mike wailed for days; you could hear him just as you'd get within sight of his front window. Screaming and crying that he couldn't go on. His children sat on the steps and cried in the spring rain. Then they built dams on the sidewalk and splashed in them naked. Very soon they were all sick with pneumonia and their tortured coughing blended with the sound of Mike's wailing. One day a car came from the children's welfare division and took every single one of them away. Between double shifts, Daddy came home for dinner and wondered out loud who might have tipped the county off. Cool teutonic stare.

One thing about my father that you'd better get straight: he was a worker. Never missed a shift. Forty years in the mill and never once late. That was my dad. When he was trying to make a point during dinner, he'd lean towards all of us, fork in hand, and say: "Work is work." I can still see him – black shiny hair and powerful gnarled hands waving in all directions while he tried to instill in his children the value of work. "Nobody in this world takes care of you; you got to work. This is the golden land; you work, you can get anything you want." He really believed it; he lived it. After all, didn't he have adorable children who were seen and not heard, a big Buick, a house, many friends, and a beautiful wife? He sure did.

His colorful friends filled our house with laughter. Their names intrigued me; they were melodious and the sound of them made me smile. I used to say them to myself when I was all alone and they kept me company. They still do. Names like Moses Isaac, Tony Calderone, Blackie Lamendola, Nicky Petrovsky, and Joe Jablonsky – "Jabbo" for short. They treated my mother with respect and admiration; they never came to our house empty handed. They'd bring specialties from their own homes: things like pierogies, sauerkraut, Easter bread, or Kielbasa. They would come for breakfast after the hoot owl shift and they were never too tired to toss us into the air. Then they would sit down and eat huge quantities of whatever was put before them, swearing it was the best breakfast they had ever eaten. And it was, too.

When Daddy came home from work in the morning, he always produced some treat for us from his coal dusted workpants. Sometimes a carton of strawberry milk with seeds in it or wintergreen Lifesavers – the kind that spark when you crunch them under the covers. He never forgot about his five out of six children. See, the fourth one died before he was born. That was my brother Layton – dead in the seventh month of my mother's pregnancy, blood polishing the floor like a skating rink. My father was on daylight shift then; it was before we had a telephone and my mother was home alone with Dostoevsky, Jack Lalayne, and a son who wouldn't live. He just wouldn't live.

Daddy came home in the afternoon, I think it was Jabbo with him that day, and found her collapsed on the floor. He picked her up and carried her to the car and Jabbo drove them to the hospital. It was good that Jabbo was there, see, to help fill out the forms. The nurses didn't understand why Mr. Carabello would be admitting Mrs. Unverzagt and Daddy was in no state to explain. He cursed the hospital and the doctors, then put his head in his hands and cried and cried, until he was only carrying coals to New Castle. But he never saw her cry and he could never tell her, no, he could never say that his tears were not just for their son, but because of the fear that she would die, too, and leave him alone.

A year and a half later, I came along. It was a bad year; everyone says so. My mother's father died and my father was on strike at the mill. At night he talked with his friends about the importance of setting up a sindacato – a union – and during the day he picked potatoes to support his family. Later on, he would sneer: "The only work dumber than millwork is farmwork. You stick a plant in the ground. You wait. Maybe it grows, maybe it don't. Drive you crazy worrying about it. Really dumb." I don't know; I never tried it. I just took his word for it. Like a lot of other things, I just took his word for it.

Like work. I took his word for that. My oldest brother took to the mills like a duck to water. My brother Kevin, now he was another story. He lived on his looks. On high school graduation day, he yawned in response to our father's anxious inquiry and said "But Dad, I just don't want to work.. Why waste time in somebody else's mill?" Daddy was speechless. Then he roared "Don't want to work? Don't want to WORK?"

He couldn't get over it, after all, any work was better than no work. But after a few years of millwork, Kevin became a history teacher. That was fine with Daddy; it was still work in any case, although work with less pay was something he couldn't understand.

One day, my mother informed all of us that she needed different work. She had a plan: she wanted to be a nurse, a psychiatric nurse, she said, and she wanted Daddy to lend her the money for college. Daddy was silent for a minute, then he said: "Why not? Everybody needs more work." We ate spumoni to celebrate. My father could not refuse her anything; he could never get over what a prize he had won somehow. So he gave her the money and she was, of course, a straight-A student and graduated with honors and all that. She paid back every penny too.

Then finally it was my turn to go down to Jane Street. My turn to go down the green hall of the administration building of Works One, turn the grimy knob and fill out the forms. There was no interview; who needed an interview? They expected me; my brothers and my father had paved the way. I looked at my reflection in the dusty office window and was not satisfied with what I saw staring back at me: there were my mother's eyes, so serious under a furrowed brow. And there were her strong, evenly-set teeth. But the smile, that was my father's. He had the kind of smile, easy and quick, that took you right to the shores of the sunny Sicily he never knew. But something in my face was missing, something wasn't there yet.

That same night, I started work on the hoot owl shift. My oldest brother was there to show me what to do. He and my father's friends watched out for me, taught me little tricks like how to hold the shovel so my back didn't get tired so fast. It was hot, exhausting work and I loved it. I loved the feel of the gloves on my fingers and the smoothness of the shovel in my hands. As a child, I had raced to the corner to meet my father after work so I could carry his big steel lunchbox and thermos. Now I had my own and a hard hat and steel-toed boots too. At break time, around 3:00 in the morning, I would slip outside to drink Maxwell House and watch the city begin to stir. The smokestacks seemed to go on forever in my mind; I couldn't imagine the end of that red-gold mill valley of molten steel.

But I could see across the river to where the tallest educational building in the world stood on the Pitt campus. It seemed to beckon to me through the smokey haze that always surrounded it. I couldn't imagine the end of the Allegheny valley, but at work I spent hours imagining the life of the mind, the life my mother dreamed of, the life my father would never know. I made it my life. Slowly, at first. I'd study on my breaks; everybody would leave me alone. It was their way of helping. Daddy's friend, Tony, would pour me a cup of steaming coffee, peer into my notebook and say "That's it, that's it, you no die like this," waving his hand at the black mill. And I knew I wouldn't. Degree after degree came my way, until finally Daddy said "Reading is good, I guess, but ain't you carrying coals to New Castle by now?"

3:00 a.m. Break time in a glowing red-gold valley. My glass is empty. But the world is not a blur and the Moldau has ceased to flow. Outside my window, I know there is green grass; I know there is a starry sky. Hundreds of letters have been sent; I know I promised. But tonight I want to tell her, I have to tell her, about all those nights in footy pajamas when the sky was orange, and all those colorful names I knew, and how I learned about love and work from them. And I have to tell her, she has to know, that even though she never sees them, there are so many tears, so many fears that she will really leave me. And so I put pen to paper and rush to carry more bituminous bits to where they are already stacked in neat piles.

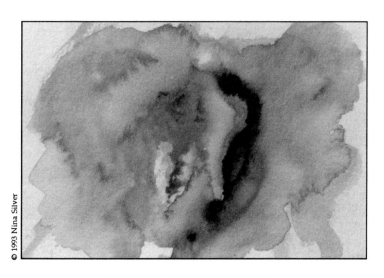

PELVIS WITH YONI

OF MY OWN ACCORD

Pam McArthur

A job at the Registry of Motor Vehicles is about as dull as they come. Most days, I watched glumly as customers spilled into my little cubicle. I'd check their eyes – "Read line six" – and take their money. They'd grumble about the long wait, and sit in a straight, wooden chair to have their picture taken. In five minutes, they'd have their new driver's license, and I'd be three or four people down the line, saying "Line six."

There was no way I could've known that particular Tuesday afternoon was going to be any different. I had been snapping pictures and silently counting the years until my retirement, just the same as usual, and I barely looked at the woman who stood at the counter around two o'clock. I'd already processed over a hundred licenses that day, so I was well into my routine, and I scarcely noticed when she read line six in a mellifluous, lightly accented voice.

I didn't even glance at her as I took her money; I was too busy trying to calculate whether I could retire at sixty or would have to wait until sixty-five, when the pension would be better. I motioned her to the chair for her photo and barely noticed the throaty chuckle with which she seated herself. The words that followed, however, did pierce my stupor.

"An attractive woman like you," she was saying, "should be on *this* side of the camera sometimes."

I looked at her sharply. All Motor Vehicle employees are suspicious of humor, and at my age – close to retirement no matter how I figured it – I was not expecting anyone to call me attractive. So I frowned at her, only to find myself looking into a warm, open face, the mouth curving upward loosely, the brown-flecked eyes dancing with mischief. The strong lines of her face looked vaguely familiar.

I allowed myself the barest smile as I flashed the camera at her, but I made no reply. She must have realized I thought she was joking. As she picked up her new license she said, "I meant it. Have you never had your picture taken professionally?"

I laughed outright at that, my memory storing the tantalizing inflections of her voice. She spoke English with ease, but also with that light accent that spoke of more exotic climates. Perhaps somewhere in the Mediterranean, I thought.

My laughter died as I remembered where I was, and I turned from the woman and called, "Next!" The afternoon dawdled on to its natural end. At five o'clock I sighed with relief and sat down. I closed my eyes tiredly, but after a few seconds, started up in surprise. Before me was that oddly familiar face, the smile, the laughing brown eyes; and I knew instinctively that the woman had not come back because of a problem with her driver's license.

"No," she said, laughing aloud as if she had read my thoughts. "I have come to make you a proposition. You have had the pleasure of taking my photograph, and now I should like the pleasure to take yours. You will allow me, yes?"

I didn't know what to say. I couldn't tell if she was crazy or just foreign. But she didn't seem dangerous, and I followed her from the room. When she opened the outer door, however, and I saw a torrential downpouring of rain outside, I drew back. She grabbed my hand and pulled me outside, yelling "Run! Run!" and I found myself racing after her, rainwater sluicing down my face. We turned a corner and galloped down a street I didn't recognize.

Splashing in and out of puddles, skin-soaked and breathless, we sped down a walkway and burst through the door of an old brick house. Laughing, she shook herself, sending clear drops of water spinning from the dark filigree of her hair. She looked at me where I stood gasping and giggling, dark rain-puddles swimming out from my feet onto the soft brown carpeting of the hallway. "Wait," she commanded, and I stood in silence while she padded down the hall.

Returning a moment later, she handed me a long robe of

thick terrycloth and a warm bathtowel. She ushered me into a nearby room, and left me alone while I dropped my clothes, dried myself luxuriously, and slid into the robe. I was surprised to find that it fit me perfectly.

When she returned, she was dressed in a robe identical to mine. She gestured around the room, at the sparse appointments which I had already taken in: under the large windows, a bed covered with a spread of blended blues and grays; and, in the opposite corner, an oak table covered with cameras and photographs. Photographs also tacked carelessly to the walls, and stacked in a pile by the door.

"Welcome," she said softly. I felt an unexpected pang as I looked around; the room brought back a long-forgotten dream of mine, to be a photographer. I grimaced at the thought of my days spent taking pictures of the silent stream of people who filed past me, when once I had dreamed of far different scenery for my lens.

"Come," she interrupted my thoughts, "we must not have the face like this." Tenderly she stroked my cheeks, my lips, coaxing a smile out of my down-turned mouth. Her touch was simple and unassuming, the way children touch; the way I had not touched since I was a child. Suddenly, under her fingers my face flushed hot, my breath quickened, and I had to turn away.

"I'm too old for all that running," I mumbled to explain my shortness of breath.

"Too old! Why, I'm just as old as you!"

I looked at the face radiating vitality, the strong hands that had just touched me, and I smiled a little forlornly. "I don't think so. Why, I'm fifty-seven years old."

She nodded gently at that, almost as if she had already known, but she made no reply. Turning from me, she lifted a camera off the table and started adjusting the lens. She peered over the camera and raised one elegant eyebrow at me. "Do you mind?"

I couldn't imagine why she wanted to photograph me. "What do you want me to do?"

She took my shoulder and turned me toward the window, so that I was leaning into the glass, leaning toward the slanting rain on the other side. I heard the click and whirr of the camera as she began to take pictures, and I hunched my shoulders uncertainly. She laughed her throat-catching laugh and began to talk to me, asking me to turn, to move, to raise an arm, lower it. I became less aware of her presence as I began to enter into the possibilities of my body. What I had long considered a creaking nuisance of corporeity became a fluid delight, fluent in all the senses.

The camera clicked continually, and at last I focused again on the woman behind it. "Where are you from? Greece?"

"Ah, Greece!" she repeated with delight. "The land of sun and salt ocean, the land of passion...." She spoke rapturously of the country I had always wanted to visit, and perhaps even to live in. I was so enchanted as she strung images for my pleasure, that I scarcely noticed she hadn't actually answered my question.

As she spoke, I turned of my own accord and raised my arm, feeling the soft slide of sleeve. Another turning brought a flash of knee and calf from their cave of cloth before the robe caught and covered them again. The camera hummed behind me, in front of me; the woman shifted my robe, roughed my hair, turned my face toward her.

I raised my eyes to her face and was caught in the radiant brown of her eyes. My hands slid to the soft folds of cloth over my breasts and I parted the robe, the camera still clicking as her breath caught, as my breath caught, as I danced forward then away again, the robe sliding over my shoulders and dropping to my hips. I felt the heat of desire even as I turned my gaze to the cold rain at the window. A distant rush of thunder masked the low moan that filled the room; I do not know whose throat it was that moaned, or who made the move to bed, but suddenly we were slung across the gray and blue comforter and keening like cats, with passion just as sharp.

Her hands, my hands, the sandpaper slide of skin on skin until skin becomes slick as midnight rain; the thunder that shook my body after lightning had split me asunder; I roared like the ocean crashing again and again against a well-loved spit of sand, the line between sand and salt water shifting continually, now ocean, now damp, sandy, sea-foam earth.

I knew she would be gone when I opened my eyes. I knew she would be gone but it didn't matter. I had been opened by love and by hunger, hunger for a mouthful of aromatic herbs or blended spice after the bland empty years of my life. I knew when I opened my eyes I would walk out the door; not at sixty-five, not at sixty, but immediately walk out the door and set my feet on every path my hunger chose.

♀

THE REPERCUSSIONS OF LOVE

Pamela Pratt

"There are places where the spirit breathes."
— Maurice Barres

My voyage circular to Maintenon (to see a chateau given by Louis XIV to his mistress, Madame de Maintenon) was important to me. Not the least of my reasons was that I am enthralled by the architecture of France in all its periods, but am fascinated even more by what has been accomplished in the name of love.

I had a lot more than that riding on the success of this day trip. Embarked upon in the middle of the afternoon in order to save a day which had been disappointing from the get go: my last day in France had to be perfect, at least passable, or the entire trip would feel like a disaster.

Even though I was fairly confident which stop on the train out of Paris would be Maintenon, it is an irritating foible of mine to seek multiple verification to ease the anxiety I always feel in countries where the answers to my questions come in a language I don't understand. I asked the cheerful nun across the aisle in my broad, flat American voice "Mai - ten - on?" I no longer try to produce a french accent, for the French are generally either confused by it or resentful of their language being spoken by an American at all, and they do not find my hand signals any more decipherable than I find their language.

I pointed out the window as I spoke to the nun, and imitated the train grinding to a halt. The train was, indeed, sliding into a station. The nun held up her hands in total non-comprehension, lifting her ample shoulders together until her chins tripled: she shook her head, mimicking "I don't know".

Panicking, I repeated the word over and over, stretching the syllables apart until "Maitenon" ceased to be a distinguishable word with meaning, even to me. An elderly woman several rows away began to shout, "Oui, oui...," shooing me off the train by waggling her hands at the train door.

We had pulled up to the platform; I could hear the conductors shouting and other doors opening up and down the train. I struggled: pushing, pulling, yanking the door handle up and down with greater and greater force; I reached through the window and tried the door handle on the outside. It would not give, either. The door handle would not budge.

I ran back into the compartment babbling, flinging my hands around, and grabbed by the arm the man seated closest to the compartment door. He did not understand, but I tugged at him so insistently that he followed me. I demonstrated what I wanted by pulling feverishly, demonically, up and down on the handle, pointing a finger at my chest and then at the platform outside, indicating *that* was where I wanted to be. He did not move, only stared at me incredulously. As the train shuddered and began, slowly, to pull away from the station, he was roused to action and began to pump the door handle himself, although not attacking it with the fervor I had. The train gathered speed. Even in my delerium I understood, finally, that should the door magically open, it was too late to jump off. I left off grasping his arm; he shrugged, gave me a sympathetic though bewildered look, and returned to his seat.

I crept back into the compartment behind him, humbled and humiliated. I did not hide my disappointment well. My face was red, my eyes grew puffy with suppressed tears, and my nose dripped my misery. The nun turned toward me and said in perfect English, "You can get off at the next station, which is Chartres, and catch a return train from there." She was an *English nun*, for God's sake, and, hearing me speak a french name place, had assumed I spoke only French. She turned to the passengers behind her and then leaned forward to the women in front, jabbering loudly in a language only I could understand, about how I had made a mistake. The compartment was full of primarily elderly French women, who clucked and murmured and shook their heads, giving me dubious looks alternated with encouraging smiles as I wiped at my eyes surreptitiously.

I did not know if the train door at Maintenon was truly jammed, or whether there was a secret to it I didn't know, but I needed to believe that it was not my own stupidity sending me on to Chartres. I had already wandered through Paris for a week feeling a perpetual angst, like a cold or cough that will not clear: I was returning to New York days ahead of schedule, discouraged by the visibly detectable sheet burns on my knee caps that I incurred roaming my tightly tucked twin bed in my sleep, searching in vain for the body of my lover. I had realized, finally, on the sixth day that it was this simple: there is finally a woman I love enough that being with her in our tiny, sunless apartment in New York is more of a thrill than gadding off to Europe on a whim. I had finally given up that defensive posture of pretending to *prefer* being alone.

It seemed as though I was going to have to add travelling alone in places where I could not communicate to the list of things I can not or will not do. That list both pains and shames me, but I have ceased to do battle with it or to dare myself over occasional defeats. I have even learned to accept certain shortcomings with grace. However, I had expected the list to grow shorter as I grew older, not mount up.

It was already four in the afternoon: I could not risk a return train to Maintenon – the chateau would probably be closed by the time I got there. I would have to make the best of Chartres. The door handle turned easily at the touch of the nun's hand. I got off the train behind the others and joined the procession advancing on the cathedral.

I drop into churches every so often for a belief test, to check in with my soul, in case it has taken to faith and overturned my atheistic upbringing. I envy the ease of faith, and even the hardness of it. I had never felt a flutter of it yet.

I am usually content to experience the *feel* of a place and leave the facts alone, but that day in Chartres I set out to learn the history, the details and meaning behind the art. I wanted to give my trip purpose: to know why Chartres was Chartres in a scholarly way. Lacking faith, I would settle thankfully for understanding belief in a cold, logical fashion.

I read the literature from the cathedral gift shop (translated into seven languages) and was made miserable by my inability to distinguish the north facade from the south, the marytr's door from the confessor's door. The central door is consecrated to Mary and the left door to the glorious Virgin and baby Jesus, details I researched and searched for, but failed to identify or differentiate. There was no glossary to define for me a tympan, a flying buttress, a splay, nor even a lintel. I could not find my way around the architecture of faith without these words. Even so, a quote from Andre Maurois sent me hope that I would find what I was looking for here – he wrote: "The cathedral is a theological treatise. All these 'Notre Dames' which stand in the principal towns of France are the ascension of the soul toward heaven. There is in the world no temple more intrinsically spiritual than Chartres cathedral." This promise of enlightenment influenced my path and led me willingly into the cathedral proper.

Inside, all I could see, while I waited for my eyes to adjust to the dimness, were the candles flickering halfway down one aisle. I tiptoed over and sat in a back row, careful not to disturb several small women in black who sat hunched and praying in the rows closest to the candles. I felt obvious: an imposter, an intruder. I sat still a long time: until the day fell away from me and I felt reclaimed by the goodness of spirit. I was moved by the women who's backs I watched, envying the strength of their belief; by the priest who came to clear the candle stubs away, and by the withered faces that turned toward him as he tended to these votive offerings. Women left quietly and were replaced by more of their kind. The only sound, besides a gutted candle falling occasionally into the tray below, was the chinking sound of one, two, or five franc pieces falling into the wooden offerings box from the hands of these women, before they reached for a candle and, lighting it from one already there, placed it on its spike and added their prayers.

The cathedral no longer felt gloomy: the light appeared to be growing brighter instead of dimmer, uninfluenced by the evening approaching faintly through the stained glass windows. After I had been sitting still for an hour, or even longer, for I had lost my sense of time, a young, modishly dressed man, much like me, approached boldly, took a long candle, the five franc kind, lit it and took his place in the front row with casual, unconcerned confidence. The women never gave him more than a cursory glance as he took his rightful place amongst them. I thought that if this young man could join the front row without disturbing anyone, then perhaps I had a right to be there as well. I crept up to the second row, watching the light pouring forth from the candles. Looking up, I could see the roof of the cathedral, so many, many feet overhead, clearly and brightly lit in that one spot above the candles, just as though a strong searchlight were trained upon it.

I imagined that the mother of the young man had cancer and the doctors had renounced all hope. I thought it had to be something that terrible to make a young man pray like this, to believe like this.

I thought about my lover's parents who will not speak my name, who thrust their daughter from them in shame when she told them of our love – all in the name of their faith. I thought how my lover comes home in tears the nights her mother has called her at work to say she has lit candles for her daughter to leave me and my lesbian ways. I thought of how my lover lives with the last words her father has ever said to her: "You're disgusting," ringing in her ears.

We had thought that time would bring them around. It hasn't. As long as they refused to understand that love of their daughter is our common language, I had thought there was nothing further I or we could do. I saw, suddenly, another way. Since they would not come to me, I would go to them.

For the first time in my life I feel at home in a church. I watch the ritual carefully now, to see what to do for sure, so I won't appear as if I don't belong. The chink of my money in the five franc box is loud. I light my candle and ease it down on its iron spike: I choose the site carefully. I sit in the front row, watching my candle, watching it's beam rise to the roof of the cathedral until it lights the way beyond that, to a pale, cloudless, blue sky. I feel my message travel through time and space as though these things are not boundaries holding us in place. I speak to her parents in the language that they know and I hear them hearing me: I see the mother pause in her ironing for just a second; I see the father in the basement, nail in one hand, the movement of his hammer raised to strike arrested for one heartbeat, before he brings it thud, down on the nail.

I don't question what has happened. I don't ask God if I now believe, if that belief will last, or what all of this means. I don't ask

---
⟨♀⟩
---

how long it will take for my prayer to be answered and I don't wonder how I know that it <u>will</u> be. My hand reaches for the handle of a door that had remained always closed to me, and the door swings open effortlessly. Looking for hope and charity, I have come upon something else.

THE BALLAD OF MOTHER FARGO

X. P. Callahan

As long as I knew her, Loretta Fargo's mother had her upper story for rent, if you know what I mean. I mean like: THIS SPACE VACANT. Like somebody shot the dots off her dice before she ever passed Go. She used to sit day in and day out and half the night in front of the TV, wearing her Peck and Peck suit and her little red pumps, just swinging her foot and smoking like a two-dollar steak. She only watched one channel – WFOG, no kidding. I guess it got that name because the station is right down next to the river where the fog can get so thick sometimes you can't even see your face in front of you. WFOG comes on the air at six in the morning and stays on till midnight and Mrs. Fargo never missed a minute, God only knows why. They show the same program all day long and all that ever happens on it, except for the flag and the national anthem at dawn and sign-off, is the camera moving real slow back and forth and back and forth over these dials that show the time and the barometer and the wind direction, with background music – stuff like "I Feel Pretty" on the xylophone, or maybe Mantovani doing "American Pie," and why they want to waste music like that on such a dumb show is beyond me but to each his own. Maybe Mrs. Fargo thought that if she kept watching those weather dials every minute, she'd have advance warning of the next big twister blowing in from Kansas. Like she could just sit there and know all about it and take herself out of harm's way, maybe click those red shoes together and say, "There's no place like home, there's no place like home" – whatever planet that was. But there she sat, just puffing away and dropping sparks and ashes, and burning holes in her skirt. I'm surprised her hair didn't go up in smoke, too, with all the spray she put on it. Now, *there* was a do! It looked like a soufflé that somebody threw over her head to cool. Mrs. Fargo smoked enough Salems to keep R. J. Reynolds in business all by herself. Her lungs must have looked like the one the Cancer Society keeps in a pickle jar to show every summer at the Hamilton County Fair. Anyway, maybe it's a good thing she took all those pills and checked out early, before the Big C got her number.

When Loretta came down to get me that day – I remember it was October, because Loretta had just moved in upstairs, right after she broke up with Corrine, and I defy anybody to prove I had anything to do with that – anyway, when Loretta comes downstairs looking about as nervous as a long-tailed cat in a room full of rockers, I figure this is just going to be one more rerun of all the other times. The thing is, Mrs. Fargo had this real knack for knowing when Loretta was going to be coming off something like a thirty-six-hour shift at Good Samaritan. She'd wait till just about half an hour before, and then she'd o.d. – Valium, Haldol, Dalmane, it didn't matter what. One time she even ate Drano, for God's sake. And just before she was going to pass out she'd call Loretta's answering machine. Meanwhile, Loretta'd be dragging herself home from the hospital, and all she wants in the whole wide world is a cup of hot Ovaltine. Imagine that – a brain surgeon drinking Ovaltine! You know, Loretta's so bright you practically have to use sunglasses just to look at her. Anyway, whenever Loretta got home, the first thing she always did was check her messages, and if there was going to be trouble it always sounded like this: "Loretta, *dear*, you'll never *guess* what I did *this* time!" And then there'd be all this crazy cackling, with an echo and a whole lot of static because Mrs. Fargo had a speakerphone so she'd never have to pick herself up from in front of the TV if she didn't feel like it. Now, Loretta's so kindhearted she won't even smack her own lips, so of course whenever she hears that voice on her machine she's got to drag herself back out of the house and over to her mom's, and then there's the paramedics and the stomach pump, and as sure as a goose goes barefoot, the next afternoon there's Mrs. Fargo sitting up in her bed at Good Sam like the Queen of Sheba, watching WFOG and hollering for room service like she's at the

Waldorf-Astoria. Like she hasn't got a care in the world except for wondering when one of the candy stripers is going to paint her toenails pink for her. She's happy. She's fixed it so Loretta won't get any sleep for another thirty-six hours. I've got to hand it to her – Mrs. Fargo had great timing. Not the last time, though.

Now, wouldn't you think, with that eighteen-hour weather watch every day, Mrs. Fargo might have had some kind of inside track on local meteorological conditions? Like maybe she'd be able to figure out that if it's raining hard enough the Columbia Parkway is going to flood and the other neurosurgery resident is going to be two hours late relieving Loretta? Anyway, when Loretta and I let ourselves into Mrs. Fargo's house that day, I thought it was just another false alarm because Mrs. Fargo's sitting back as calm as a cantaloupe in her Queen Anne chair and she's staring at the TV screen. Her mouth is hanging open and the light from the television is splashing on her face and making her look like one of those blue ceramic goldfish they keep on the bottom of the live-lobster tank at the Howard Johnson's restaurant out on the interstate. I mean, she looks pretty much the same way she always does except she isn't smoking. But she isn't breathing either, and when I turn around, Loretta has a look on her face like a bowling setup with half the pins knocked over. It's funny what stays in your mind. I remember there was this old pink sponge, all dried up and hard enough to crack, sort of half-balancing on the edge of the highboy. I remember thinking Mrs. Fargo liked Callard & Bowser toffee. So anyway, they covered Mrs. Fargo up and carried her out, and the neighbors were all standing around the driveway not saying anything, and it was 2:47 and the rain was over and the temperature was fifty-four degrees with the barometer rising and the wind coming out of the southwest at seventeen miles per hour, and the music on WFOG was 101 Strings playing "I Want to Hold Your Hand." One of the paramedics went back in the house for the empty bottle of phenobarb and stuck it in a little blue plastic bag, and I'm real glad Loretta didn't see him do it. She was feeling bad enough as it was, especially on account of prescribing those pills herself.

The next day, even though Corrine still wasn't officially

speaking to me yet, she let up and helped me make all the arrangements with the two Schuster brothers that run the Perpetual Light crematory. Corrine can be as stubborn as a mule in molasses and most times she's mean enough to bite her own behind, if you care to know my opinion, but I guess she understood that we're Loretta's whole family now, along with Wanda and Janey and Little Bit. There was a Mr. Fargo once but he went out for a long lunch maybe twenty years ago and we couldn't have found him if we tried. Which Loretta said we shouldn't bother to do in any case, so that was that.

Did you ever hear somebody sing in a voice so pretty you got a lump in your throat? That's how Janey sounded at the service. She's got this scratched-up old guitar and all this long straight shiny hair parted right down the middle that makes her look like a folksinger anyway, so she'd have it made if she ever wanted to quit her service-rep job at Cincinnati Bell and go commercial, which she could easily do because Wanda has an uncle or a cousin or something that used to make deliveries for a record distributor out of Louisville, so there are strings to be pulled. As a matter of fact, Janey could start in right now because Little Bit is the deejay at Satan's Lair and she runs the live talent show there on Friday nights and she's forever going over to Wanda and Janey's and trying to get Janey to stop in there and do a few numbers, but with Janey it's always no-no-no she can't. So then Bit gets mad, and when she gets mad she'll say something real blunt, like "Janey, just because you're fat, that doesn't mean you cannot sing for the public." Now, this is where Wanda jumps in and says Janey is *not* fat, and Janey says she is so but that has nothing to do with her not wanting to sing at Satan's, and by the way, she wishes some people would just butt right the hell on out of some other people's business, thank you very much. So then Little Bit slams out of the house and Wanda stomps into the bedroom. Or if it's late enough in the day Wanda will head for the fridge and open herself a Little King. But anyway, Janey does have a real beautiful voice, and the way she sang "You Light Up My Life" at the crematory for Mrs. Fargo was enough to make the Schuster brothers cry too if they didn't happen to be such a slippery couple of cold fish. It was just like at the mortuary when my grandma died, and this bald-headed stiff is pulling a long face they taught him at funeral school and trying to make everybody line up for the last look so he can hustle Grandma out to the hearse, and meanwhile my mom's lip is quivering so bad she looks to be about four years old, and my dad even had to go out by himself for a minute to cry in the lobby. I'm telling you, it's a crime the way these people operate. I mean, wouldn't you think, with all the money they're raking in – and you can tell, because those two fish-faces are so crooked they practically have to screw their socks on, and they've got a couple of big old Lincoln Continentals parked right outside the crematory, and all that red velvet brocade wallpaper in the chapel sure doesn't come cheap, and even their receptionist has that glamorous look, with all this frosted hair and fingernails out to here and patent-leather shoes with these skinny little high heels that are so spiky you could stand her on her head and play ringtoss with Cheerios, and you can bet the farm she doesn't go home at night and fix herself a Spam omelette for supper either – anyway, with all that money, wouldn't you think Zane and Herschel Schuster could maybe look around a little and find something *nice* to stick Mrs. Fargo's ashes in? Well, after the service, they send us out of the chapel and tell us to wait in this little room off to the side, with green walls and elevator music, and a little while later here they both come, one cold fish slithering right alongside the other, one on each side of this white cardboard box with the lid taped on – and we're talking regular old ugly brown masking tape here, forget Scotch Magic Transparent. Now, to look at this box, you couldn't tell if what was inside was somebody's mother's mortal remains or a new pair of Converse All-Stars. For all I know, the stupid thing might be a contribution from Ms. Spiky Heels out at the front desk. Anyway, here come these two slimy guys with poker faces, and they're carrying this dumb ordinary shoebox like it's some kind of sunken treasure chest that got hauled up in the same net with them, and they slide on over and hand it to Loretta, and then all of a sudden I couldn't stop seeing Mrs. Fargo swinging her foot and smoking her Salems, with all those cigarette butts spilling out of the ashtray and all over the floor, and I got to kind of wondering how far around the world they'd reach if you could line them all up filter to filter, even if you only counted up the ones from the three years I'd known Loretta, and all I could think to say about Mrs. Fargo was "ashes to ashes," so I didn't say it. Herschel Schuster did, though. We grabbed Mrs. Fargo and got the hell out.

We all went back to Loretta's place, which does happen to be right upstairs from mine, and if Corrine doesn't like that she has only herself to blame, because if you ask me Corrine did have a few other choices besides practically having a basket of kittens and kicking Loretta out, but try telling Corrine that. Loretta put her mother on the mantel and Wanda opened up a bottle of Jack Daniel's while Janey and Little Bit were shoving Loretta's books and clothes and magazines out of the way for everybody to sit down. So we all sat around not saying much, just drinking and looking at that awful white box. It was so quiet you could hear the temperature drop. Pretty soon Little Bit said she had to leave for her gig at Satan's, and Wanda and Janey left too. So then it was just Corrine and Loretta and me. Corrine kept looking like she wanted to say something but was making an all-out effort to be too nice to say it, and as far as I was concerned she could save her breath anyway because I didn't need to know what she thought. Probably that just as soon as she left, Loretta and I would be on each other like rabbits, and I suppose that's why Corrine hung around till almost midnight. When she finally took off, I stayed a little while with Loretta. Then I gave her a big long hug and went downstairs. I could hear her crying all night long and it was real hard not to go up there, just crawl in bed next to her and hold her, but I wasn't going to give Corrine the satisfaction.

A few days after that, Loretta went back to work, and the whole time she was gone I kept hearing music coming from upstairs. I thought she must have left her radio on by mistake but I didn't feel right about just letting myself in and turning it off, so when I heard her come in a couple days later I went up to ask her about it. I knocked, and she told me to come in, and there she is drinking Jack Daniel's on the couch next to her mother, and the two of them are watching WFOG. I poured the whole bottle down the sink and fixed Loretta some Ovaltine. Then I talked to her a little while and called Janey, and Janey came over and took Mrs. Fargo away. Loretta cried some, but it was the kind of crying like when you tell little kids they're not allowed to do something they're scared to do anyway, such as go over Niagara Falls in a barrel. In Loretta's case, I told her she could not get drunk and watch the TV weather dials with her dead mother and then show up in the O.R. and fiddle around with other people's brains. Maybe somebody should have done some fiddling around with hers, I don't know. But I'll tell you one thing. I sure as hell wasn't going to stand around and watch her mess up her neurosurgery residency even if certain people who were supposed to be her nearest and dearest had seen fit to throw her out in the cold at a critical point in her professional development – but I won't mention any names.

Mrs. Fargo would have been just fine at Wanda and Janey's except that Wanda was starting to get into the supernatural. That wasn't too bad at first. It just meant you couldn't go over there without whacking your head on some big stupid crystal that was hanging in the doorway, or maybe Wanda would have to check out your aura before she'd let you in. But pretty soon Wanda hears about black magic. Now, I don't know where she'd been for the past twenty-five years. I mean, maybe she grew up in a disadvantaged home where they didn't let her look at "The Twilight Zone" and "The Outer Limits." Anyway, she hears about black magic and it's this real big deal. I swear, I truly think she lost her mind a little. Before long she's muttering about psychic assassins and evil discarnate entities. She's drawing protective pentangles on the kitchen linoleum with special eight-dollar chalk because her bridgework is conducting X-rated transmissions from a secret network of Tibetan incubi and she's sure Mrs. Fargo is responsible. Then one day a four-hundred-dollar electric bill comes and Janey finally blows her top. It turns out that Wanda was leaving the furnace and downstairs lights on all night long to try and plug the leaks in Mrs. Fargo's ectoplasm or some damn thing. Well, that did it. Mrs. Fargo got moved out to the garage.

It was damper than a swamp out there and darker than a stack of black sheep and it must have been about three weeks afterwards that Little Bit happened to hear about it. She felt sorry for Mrs. Fargo and wanted to take her home but we didn't know about that because Bit had been heard to call her Mom-in-the-Box and we thought that was kind of disrespectful.

We never told Loretta about that, naturally. But when you stop and think about it, it was pretty disrespectful to send Mrs. Fargo out to live with the snowblower, and it was also disrespectful to dump her in a shoebox in the first place, so we thought Mrs. Fargo could do worse than go stay with Little Bit and we said okay.

Little Bit got Loretta's mom all set up nice and cozy on top of the kitchen radiator, to dry her out, and I guess they got along all right because pretty soon Bit starts calling her Mother Fargo. You'd drop over and ask what's doing and she'd say she was communing with Mother Fargo. Little Bit can be weird sometimes. I mean, she writes poetry and that's okay by me but she never uses any capital letters or periods or anything and none of it rhymes and that's not the way I learned but I guess it's still a free country. Anyway, things are going along fine till one day Bit tells Janey and me that Mother Fargo has been doing the laundry. Janey says, "What laundry? Her shroud?" Janey's not really sarcastic. It's just that she was still burned up about Wanda and the electric bill. Little Bit says, "No, silly, *my* laundry," and she says Mother Fargo's not only washing her clothes, she's pressing and folding them too. Janey says, "That's nice," and she tells Bit she's got to run, but first she makes her promise not to say anything to Wanda about the laundry. To this very day I don't know what to think about it myself and I get a headache if I try. I mean, first they're growing babies in test tubes, and now I see on that science show that all the water in the world probably comes from thirty-foot-wide snowballs from outer space, so why shouldn't Little Bit's washerwoman be a dead person in a shoebox? What do I know? I'm no Einstein, so I sure don't have all the answers, and I was truly glad that Bit and Mrs. Fargo were getting along so good and I wished them all the best, but all I needed was not to know any more than I absolutely had to about whatever the hell was going on over there and I'd be happy too, and that's what I told Little Bit.

And I suppose that would have been the end of it except that a couple months later – it's Saint Patrick's Day by now – Loretta and I happen to drive over to Satan's to have a few beers and catch up with some people we know, including Donny and Fred, and I'm not one of those that say the boys should never be allowed in our place but I sure as hell wish they'd use their own toilet because there's nothing worse than pee drops on the seat. Well, to tell you the truth, there is something worse, and why the boys' toilet doesn't have doors is something I for one will never understand, because if it did then this one particular little problem would be solved, although when you stop and think about it there's also a lot to be said for the privacy of your own home if you're a consenting adult, but it's a crazy world and I'm not one to hold a grudge against the whole bunch of them just because a few don't even have the manners of uneducated barnyard animals so we sat down at Donny and Fred's table and ordered ourselves some green beer. It was only nine o'clock, but the place was packed. We waved to Little Bit over in the deejay booth and she yelled something back but we couldn't hear because the music was so loud. The dance floor was jammed. I settled back to watch, and I put my arm across the back of Loretta's chair – I swear, I wasn't even touching her – and that's when I saw Corrine on the other side of the bar, and she saw Loretta and me at the same time. Corrine must have been drinking Windex, that's how easy it was to see right through her. I mean, the woman's as dumb as a box of rocks to begin with. If brains were dynamite, Corrine wouldn't even have enough to blow her nose. First she gives us both a look you could pickle a radish in. Then she starts cozying up to this woman Robin that's sitting next to her. I just had to laugh. Robin thinks she's hot enough to fry her own spit, and here's Corrine pawing and cuddling and trying to look about as worked up as a cat at a mouse show, making like she's into this hot and heavy thing with Robin. But everybody knows Robin's always running her mouth and I happen to know from personal firsthand experience that if you make it with Robin even one time the whole world hears about it before the wet spot dries. I'm not kidding, Robin's vibrator must be hooked up to United Press International. Now, as far as I knew, there was nothing going out over the wire about those two yet, but anyway, if Corrine wanted Robin she could have her as far as I was concerned. At least Corrine would have someplace warm to stick that big nosy face of hers instead of up in other people's business all the time, and I was just about to say so to Loretta when I noticed that Loretta wasn't looking at Corrine and Robin at all. She was staring real hard in Little Bit's direction, and I couldn't see why right away because Bit's just standing over there with her headphones and turntable, just sort of bopping and jumping along like she always does, but then I take a closer look and I think, Oh shit, because on the ledge next to the deejay booth there's this white box, and the music is so loud the box is jumping right along with Little Bit.

You know how Aretha sings "Respect" and she does that part that goes R-E-S-P-E-C-T? Well, she only got as far as the second E and then there's this big *scree-e-e-e-ch* and it took a couple seconds for everybody to stop dancing because there's still this bump-bump-bump-bump, but it's only Loretta pounding Little Bit into the turntable. Bit's mike is still on, and she's going "Come *on*, Loretta, don't you want to just *talk* about it?" And clear as a bell, Loretta says, "No, thank you, I would rather kiss a pig." Well, when I heard that, I couldn't help but look over at Corrine again, but I couldn't look for long because the crowd starts pushing me back, it's parting like the Red Sea, and here comes Loretta marching right down the middle with that white box under her arm. Everybody's staring at her, real quiet, and Loretta's walking tall right out of Satan's just like Marshal Dillon at Miss Kitty's Saloon.

All the way over to Good Sam, Little Bit was moaning and clutching at her ribs in the back seat of Donny's station wagon, just blabbering on about how she never meant any harm but Mother Fargo was getting so lonely at night and isn't it best to get out among other people when you feel that way? I don't know about that and I really didn't have time to think about it either because as soon as we walk into Emergency we've got another problem. There's Corrine standing right up next to the admissions desk with this young cop, and how she rounded him up so fast I'll never know. Maybe she put out an APB on Robin's vibrator. Anyway, there she is, and she points her bony finger at Little Bit and says,"This is the woman that wants to press charges." Can you imagine? Well, Bit just gives her this real evil look and says no, there's no problem, she only wants to get taped up and get on home if that's not inconveniencing anybody too much. I left Bit with Donny and Fred and told her I'd call in the morning. Then I let the cop drive me home, on account of Loretta taking the car, and it's just a damn good thing I was in the company of an officer of the law, too, because otherwise Corrine would have been rolling out of Emergency under a big white sheet, with a tag on her toe that said ONE DEAD BITCH.

I told the cop happy Saint Patrick's Day and thanks for the ride, and he said I should forget it and took off. Then I turned around, and just like they say, I think my heart really did skip a beat, because I saw Loretta's car parked all weird way up our driveway with all the windows rolled up and the engine running and the headlights shining into the back yard and I thought, Oh Jesus Christ, and it seemed like it took a whole sixty seconds before I could get my legs to work right but then I ran like hell to drag her out. Only she wasn't in there. She was in the yard, just boohooing in the high beams on her hands and knees, and she's trying to shove the whole damn box down this tiny little hole she dug with a garden trowel like she's burying a pet hamster or something. And when she sees me she starts crying even harder and she says it's all been going on long enough already and she can't take it anymore.

I took the box out of her hands and got most of the dirt shook off it. Then I got Loretta's car parked right and told her to come in the house. We went upstairs and I fixed her some Ovaltine and I said, "Look, Loretta, I know you want this done with, and I agree with you, but I've got a better idea if you can wait a couple more months." And I promised her we'd all go out on my boat just as soon as the weather warmed up some, and she said okay, and after that I took her downstairs and tucked her into my bed and cuddled up next to her for the whole night, because I decided right then and there that I didn't give a good goddamn anyhow what Corrine thought and I never would again.

So anyway, right after Memorial Day, everybody's upstairs at Loretta's and we're all ready to go down and get in the car when the phone rings. Loretta picks it up and she says it's Corrine and Corrine wants to go too and can she bring Robin. Well, it sure wasn't me or Loretta that told Corrine about it and I bet it wasn't Janey or Little Bit either, so it had to be Wanda because by that time Wanda was into this stuff called Transformations and she was running around practically foaming at the mouth to forgive everybody for any little old thing whether they even did it or not. I felt like saying something about how maybe Robin could radio ship-to-shore just in case our small craft got into some kind of distress but instead I just said, "What the hell, but they can drive their own damn selves." So off we go, just the five of us, down the Columbia Parkway to Kellogg Avenue, just cruising right on down along there past the waterworks and the nuke towers, out east towards River Downs. In twenty minutes or so we turn off and head south a little ways to the marina, and pretty soon there she is – my boat, the Tiger III.

You ought to see my boat. She's a beauty – Bayliner cabin cruiser, thirty-two-foot and real sleek-looking, with an inboard Chrysler motor and two steering stations, one in the cabin and one on top of the bridge, and she'll do thirty knots easy. Corrine and Robin got there first, and I just about swallowed my teeth when I spotted them. They're lolling around on the edge of the pier, just slobbering and sliding all over each other like a couple of teenage slugs, and they probably wouldn't have even noticed us except that Loretta nudges the car up real real close to them and lays on the horn. Then Loretta leans around to the back seat and says, "Wanda, forgive me for that and I'll kill you."

Well, we got all our stuff unloaded from the car. Janey had her guitar, naturally, and some flowers – real pretty mums that she ordered special – and Wanda brought Fritos and Ding-Dongs and a case of Little Kings, and I suppose asking some people to stay sober long enough to observe a solemn rite of burial at sea is about as silly as looking for a whisper in the wind, but on the other hand it was a beautiful warm day and once you get out there on the river a Little King can taste so good you wish your throat was a mile long, and besides, like Wanda said, it was a wake, wasn't it, so I just decided to button up my lip about it. Little Bit said she wanted to carry the box with Mother Fargo in it if that was all right, so I grabbed Loretta's hand and marched right on past Corrine and Robin just as bold as you please without even looking at them and we all climbed on board.

I got the motor fired up, and the propeller started turning, and then that good old Ohio River water was washing over the rudder and the Tiger III was on her way. We decided to head south a little, then east towards Coney Island, and then just see what we felt like doing. There wasn't much of a breeze and it was hot out there. I thought we were all going to get a sunburn, Loretta especially, because she was real white. And even though it was so hot, she kept shivering, so I told her to come in the cabin with me and I kept ahold of her hand while I steered.

About ten minutes out, I cut the motor and let us drift. I dug up a jacket for Loretta and we went back out on deck. It seemed like it was time. Little Bit said she wanted to read a poem. Maybe she wrote it herself, or maybe it was a real poem, I don't know, but it sure had a whole lot to say about bones and stones and the moon and I have to admit I couldn't make much sense out of it but I guess it's the thought that counts. I don't mean to say I wasn't moved by Little Bit's poem but maybe I wasn't just exactly as moved as Bit might have thought. I mean, I know she saw tears in my eyes, but that was only because Wanda lit up a stick of sandalwood incense right under my nose. Anyway, Little Bit's poem took about twenty-five minutes and then it was time for Janey to sing. She sang "You Light Up My Life" again, just like at the crematory, and then she sang that song about down by the banks of the O-hi-o. It just seemed fitting and it was so pretty I really did get real tears in my eyes that time but I blinked them all back because I didn't want to get Loretta going. So I just sat there and concentrated real hard on looking at Corrine. I don't know what the hell she was doing out there with us in the first place. I mean, she never did do much for Loretta, did she, and God knows she sure as hell never lifted a single damn one of her scrawny fingers to help Mrs. Fargo out, and by the way, who wasn't even *with* Loretta the day she found her mother passed away in that Queen Anne chair? Well, Corrine just takes this great big pull on her Yoo-Hoo Chocolate Beverage – seven people, and she only brings along one little bottle – and she stares right back at me like there's nobody and nothing in this wide world she's got to answer for, and I'm not saying it isn't the Lord's business but we'll just see what He has to say about it one of these fine days, and the sooner the better as far as I'm concerned.

And I guess it's been about two years now, or almost, but it's still like yesterday remembering what happened next. After Janey stopped singing, everybody stayed real quiet for a while. The water was slapping up against the hull of the Tiger III and that was the only sound you could hear except for people screaming every couple seconds from the Big Dipper and the Tilt-A-Whirl at the amusement park down the north bank. I wish you could see the Dipper. You can't, though, because they finally had to tear it down last fall after the termites got so bad. Anyway, Little Bit stands up and carries the box over to Loretta, and it was just like when the Marines or the Kiwanis or whoever the hell it was took that big American flag off the President and folded it all up in a fat little triangle and handed it to Mrs. Kennedy. Well, we all took a few flowers and tossed them overboard, and Wanda got her Swiss army knife out and helped Loretta cut through that stupid masking tape. So Loretta takes this big deep breath and she steps over to the starboard rail and shuts her eyes and turns the box upside down, and we're all waiting for Mrs. Fargo's ashes to kind of flutter down like little snowflakes and just drift away on down the river. Only they don't. I mean, we could have just thrown the whole shoebox in for all the damn difference it made. Too bad we didn't. We hear this little splash, and then there's Mrs. Fargo, just floating on top of the water in a nice big white lump. Just sitting out there on the Ohio River in the middle of all those mums, not moving or sinking or anything. Just *there*. Corrine says to Robin, real sneaky and quiet, "Some things *never* change." I could have hauled off and popped her one but I didn't think Loretta heard, so I let it go.

Well, we couldn't just leave Mrs. Fargo out there, could we, and I don't know how long we were supposed to wait, especially since it looked like she was fixing to spend all eternity just bob-bob-bobbing along under those red lights blinking on the WFOG-TV tower. Loretta's crying her eyes out by this time, and she's gripping the rail and looking like she just saw a ghost, which in a way I guess she did. I couldn't stand it. I ducked back in the cabin and pulled a flypole off the rack, and Wanda grabbed it and started poking at Mrs. Fargo and trying to make her sink, but no dice. I didn't know what to do. I took the pole away from Wanda and stuck it back up on the rack, and the next thing I know, I turn around and there's Corrine hanging over the side, yelling "Toodle-oo!" and chunking Loretta's mother up with a gaff hook.

She went down pretty fast after that, which was okay with the rest of us but Loretta got hysterical. Janey tried to calm her down. She sang I don't know how many verses of "Amazing Grace" and then she started back at the beginning and sang them all through again, and the whole time Loretta's bending over the rail with her mouth open and making this *maaa-maaa* sound like some kind of big baby doll. It was just horrible.

Anyway, like I said, it was a couple years ago all this happened, and I guess that's been plenty of time for me to think about it, but maybe I never will understand how life can be so weird and unfair sometimes. I suppose I should mention that ever since the first of the year Corrine has been spending two nights a week up at Loretta's and I sure don't like that one damn bit, let me tell you. I mean, wouldn't you think that after somebody pulverizes your one and only mother with a piece of heavy nautical equipment, you shouldn't invite that person to darken your door again? Like maybe you ought to consider the wisdom of your romantic involvements and follow the advice that's freely given to you by those who truly care? Now that the weather is warm again, I spend those two nights on the Tiger III. It's just me and the river out there. I stand up on the bridge just like Columbus and look over at the city lights. Last week I even sang "Amazing Grace" to myself, or at least as much of it as I could remember. It was my birthday that night, it just so happens, and I'm thirty-five years old now and I sure as hell don't know what's going to happen from here on in. I mean, maybe I should be planning to just move on out to my boat for good, I don't know. I'll tell you one thing though. Janey's not getting any younger either and it's really high time she started using her connections in the music industry. I mean it, she could be bigger than Conway Twitty and Brenda Lee all rolled up into one. I know she could write a real beautiful song about this whole damn mess, and maybe when she sang it everything would start making some kind of sense. Like when my clock radio came on in the morning, the first thing I'd hear would be Janey's song, and the whole day would come out right. It could be one of those slow numbers, with all that pretty finger-picking and stuff, and she could sing about everything that's been going on ever since Mrs. Fargo bought her one-way ticket to never-never land. I just know she'd have a big hit record, and then she could tour all over the world. Be on TV and everything. Who knows, they might even play it on WFOG. At least then maybe we could say Loretta's mother didn't take her own life in vain.

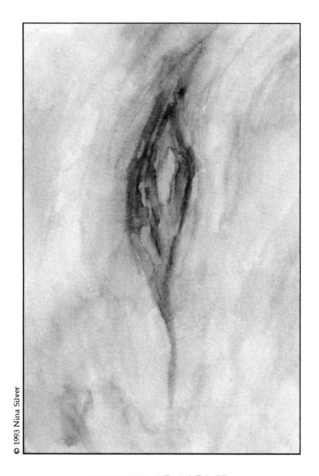

© 1993 Nina Silver

INVITING YONI

AMONG THE CREATURES OF HABIT

Dianna Hunter

Dad spent thirty-six years in the dairy business in northern Minnesota. He never would have quit, except that he died of a stroke, trying to dig out a tractor he had got stuck in a cold, wet field. Once, Dad went nineteen years without missing a single milking. That had been necessary, he said, purely economic. By 1964, he and Mom had worked so hard and had been so thrifty that they were able to pay cash for a brand new barn. They specified that the contractors should use glass blocks at even intervals in the concrete block walls. It was the smartest thing they ever did, Dad said, lightening up the barn that way.

They were always proud of my schoolwork, so when I begged to go East to college, they sent me to Haversmith. That was definitely not the smartest thing they ever did, Dad always said, sending me to a school that offered yoga for credit. He had wanted me to major in elementary ed, come home, teach in Bear Claw, and find a husband to run the farm. Instead, I designed my own major, a mixture of women's studies, ecology and theology, and came home raring to run the dairy farm myself. Dad's arguments to the contrary, that farming was not women's work, that I would be stuck here forever, that my education would be wasted, etc., were foreclosed by his death.

Now I use my education every day. When my muscles are inadequate, I figure out how to use jacks and hoists to do the job, I compost my cow manure in long, scientifically-designed piles; and I meditate in short snatches, standing between two cows. It's a unity with the universe I feel, as my rib cage is squeezed between two much more copious rib cages, rising and falling, heavy and slow, in time with the clucking of three milker machines. It's ritualistic. Fifty-two beats to the minute.

"Milk down! Air up! Milk down! Air up!" The three milkers' plastic and rubber hearts set a dependable, even tempo in the barn, until some tender-titted heifer kicks one of them into the manure or my mother comes by in theatrical silence, with two buckets hanging heavy in her hands.

This morning, when I heard the roaring of the vacuum pump rise above the soft clucking of the milkers, I knew that the milkhouse door had swung open. Shortly after that, I saw Mother coming down the white, limed aisle, carrying two ice cream pails half-full of warm milk. She stopped short, just past me, as though she had been surprised to see me there, and twirled on one heel like a soldier.

"I forget now," she said. "Does that black calf still get milk or no?"

"She's weaned," I told her, squatting so I could massage a nervous new heifer's udder, coaxing her to let down her milk. "That calf eats grain like a champ already – gonna be just like her mom."

"Which one's her mom again?"

"Lady Day!" I heard myself saying in a voice much too shrill. We had discussed the black calf's feeding, and her parentage, too, yesterday and the day before that. "Remember Lady Day?" I asked, lowering my pitch, "The one I won the dairy breeder's trophy with?"

Mother scuffled toward the calf pen in her knee-high rubber boots, muttering, so that I could barely hear her over the noise of the vacuum pump, "*You* won! All by yourself, I suppose!"

· · ·

I had the milkers on a whole new set of cows by the time Mother came back and set her empty buckets down on the limed aisle – something she always did, which drove me crazy because the lime stuck to the bottom of the buckets and got carried into the milkhouse where it would eventually rot the drainpipe, creating a problem that I – not Mother – would have to fix in fifteen or twenty years. Mother had been wearing an old flowered scarf, babushka-style. She pulled it off, fluffed her hair, and asked me, "What did you say to Arvo last night when he called?"

"That I had a cow for him to breed."

"That's all?"

"That's right. He was just returning my call because I left a message on his answering machine. How'd you know he called, anyway?"

"I happened to pick it up in the house, that's all. I didn't know you had already picked it up out here."

"Funny you didn't listen to the whole conversation then."

"Well, I was wondering...." she said, grinning the way I have seen her do so often, the same way our collie grins when we've caught him in his habitual crime of stealing eggs from the henhouse. "Why don't you go to the movies with Arvo like he asked you to? I could do the milking for you. Your Aunt Judy would come over and help me if I asked her, I'm sure. In fact, I suppose I should admit to you, I already asked her, and she said she would."

I jumped up from my crouch and scared the cow I was milking. She jumped away from me, and the four rubber cups of her milker slipped down to the end of her tits, gave a squeal, and then sucked back up, high on her tits where they belonged. The milker never missed a beat.

"That would be the Christian thing for Aunt Judy to do now, wouldn't it?" I grumbled.

"And what do you mean by that?"

I could hear the argument over religion coming, and I didn't want to have it. Mother would defend her sister's old-time fundamentalism, even though Mother herself never went to church. Like me, she was more of an animist than a Swedish Baptist. I buried my face in the jumpy cow's flank so that I wouldn't have to look at Mother while I plotted how to get her to drop the date-with-Arvo idea. Finally, I told her, with a deadpan face, "I didn't want to have to tell you this, Mom, but I think Arvo might be planning a date rape."

"No!" she said. "Why do you say that?"

"Reading between the lines a little," I said. "He wants to take me to see the latest Rocky movie, and do you know what he says to me? He says, 'A chance to see the Italian Stallion in action!'"

"That's it?"

"That's not enough, Mom? 'The Italian Stallion' he says!"

"The things you come up with!" Mother's voice was getting shrill. "Let me tell you something you obviously did not learn in fancy pants Haversmith College! There's a difference between rape and ordinary courtship, and Arvo is not such a bad guy. He's a little needy, granted. Who wouldn't be, the way Donna left him so sudden? It's not easy, you know, all the rumors going around town about her two-timing him while he's out breeding cows. Naturally, he's hurting, but sometimes those kind of guys are the ones a woman can really do something with. They know they need someone. You know what I mean!"

I looked her in the eyes and let out a whinny.

"Okay, okay! Listen, Miss College Genius, maybe he asked you to go to a dumb movie, but Arvo is no dummy around cows. All I'm saying is I'm getting tired, and I'm not going to be around forever. You need a partner on this farm!"

. . .

I heard the barn door creak and saw a puff of lime blow down the aisle. Arvo Matilla lumbered into the barn, black quilted coveralls adding even more bulk to his 200-pound body. When he spotted me, he turned in the opposite direction, toward the sheet metal breeder's record box mounted on the wall.

"Think about it," Mother whispered, before she disappeared into the milkhouse with the calf buckets.

"Which cow did you want me to breed then?" Arvo yelled in a strained voice, keeping his eyes fixed on the breeding records. He was acting strange. His normal procedure was to find out which bull I wanted him to use, then to thaw the semen, then to breed the cow, and only then to go to the record box, to mark down the breeding.

"Lady Day!" I yelled back, "Halfway down the aisle here."

"Which bull did you want me to use, then ?" he shouted, still facing the wall.

"Commando," I said, naming a high-priced bull from a company that was not the company Arvo worked for. I had bought some of Commando's semen from the Prairieland Breeders's fieldman, and I kept it stored in a liquid nitrogen tank in the milkhouse, frozen in little plastic straws that looked like swizzle sticks.

"You know..." Arvo said, still facing the wall, "...I've been making an exception for you, seeing's our families are such old friends, but I don't know if I can keep it up. Our sales manager says we shouldn't be using customer-owned semen any more. I should be selling you some of our own."

That was not good news for me, with thousands of Commando's expensive spermatazoa waiting in suspended animation in my milkhouse, but I decided to play it the Zen way – calmly. "Okay," I said, naming Arvo's company's best bull. "You got Patton?"

"Well," Arvo weaseled, still facing the wall. "He's a little expensive to keep on hand. Most people around here can't afford to use him."

"Sarge?"

"He's a little expensive, too."

"How about Emperor?"

"Same way there."

"Jesus Christ, Arvo! You expect me to breed the best cow in the county to some ten dollar bull? Have something decent on hand, if you want me to use your semen!"

I heard a high-pitched yip. At first I thought the dog had hurt himself somehow, but then I saw Arvo stomping down the center aisle toward me. His cheeks were florid, and his mouth turned down in a tight line. Like falling dominoes, the Holsteins turned their heads when they heard the "swish, swish, swish" of his coveralls. I stood up, spread my legs a little, and breathed deeply from my diaphragm, getting ready to block a punch or squeeze between the cows into the feed aisle.

Then Arvo stopped and shook his head a little, like he was trying to get some loose piece of it back into the right slot. He said, "Okay! I'll breed that cow for you, and I'll use that semen you got from Prairieland. But goddamn it! That's it! From now on, if you don't want what I got to sell, don't call me! Got it?"

"Got it," I said, almost breathless. For a minute there, I had thought he had figured out it was me who had been doing what my mother called "two-timing" him with his wife. I had been doing something with Donna, but "two-timing" was hardly the word I would have used for it. I didn't know what to call it exactly, since even "love-making" is not an adequate phrase to describe what two people do when that irrepressible sexual energy sparks between them. The way I saw it, what we did with each other was as ineffable as Donna herself, and the essence of her certainly could not be contained within the words "Arvo's wife." To me, she was the practical magician, the poetic athlete, the philosophical mechanic – a paradoxical, hard-working, creative genius who could massage the will to live back into a half-dead calf and then turn around and rewire a tractor with a jacknife and a pair of pliers.

Arvo broke my reverie, saying "Don't look so relieved! Donna was over this morning, and we talked. She still tells me things, you know. Right this minute, I would just as soon kill you as look at you! But out of respect for your mother and your cows, I won't. You got a lot depending on you."

"Oh," I said, reminding myself that the hard times in farming had left Arvo the only inseminator still working in this part of Bear Claw County.

. . .

I poked my head into the milkhouse, where Mom stood in the light fog she had created by running hot water in the cool air. I said to her, "Would you write Arvo a check for three-hundred dollars, please?" I turned around and said to Arvo, "Order us five straws of Patton, then."

He nodded and went about his business, frowning the whole time. He plopped a strawful of the contraband semen into warm water. By the time I had finished milking, Mother had Arvo's check ready. He took it, shot Commando's freshly-wakened sperm into Lady Day with his long syringe, and went back out the door. Mother washed the milkers while I climbed the ladder to the mow and dropped down several leafy bales of clover hay.

I broke the bales apart and scattered the hay in front of the cows, who were craning for it. Then I stood still, breathing deeply, taking in the sweet scent of the clover and the even sweeter exhaled breath of the masticating cows. My world was unified again and peaceful. The heartbeat of the barn had fluttered – like it does when a calf is born backwards or when a clumsy cow steps on her own tit and smashes it – but here among the creatures of habit, every disturbance is quieted by routine work and the passage of time.

It's still three weeks until the end of the January. Soon I'll ask Donna to move in with me and Mother. Mother might squawk, but what can she do? It's not as though she doesn't know about me and Donna. She's seen us laughing and mooning at each other hundreds of times. It's just hard for her to admit that she sees what's in front of her own eyes – like that dream I have all the time, where I'm trying to read but I can't quite make out the words, and then I realize that I have my eyes shut. Once Mother opens her eyes, she'll realize that Donna can be the partner we need around here. Come May, when we're fighting the heavy, wet clay, trying to get our oats planted, she'll see how handy Donna is with machinery.

I'm even hoping that Arvo will stop by for coffee once in awhile, after he gets used to the way things are.

♀

MY RASPBERRY SWEETIE AND ME

Susan B. McIver

"I want to do something really gay," Anne said.

"Like what?" I asked, throwing back the covers on our bed.

"I told you. Something really gay."

"Okay. For your birthday we'll do something really gay."

Anne took out the dogs while I fumbled for both my clothes and the meaning of her request.

I had trouble thinking of anything we did that wasn't gay. We lived on Lesbos West, alias Salt Spring Island, British Columbia. Most of our friends were gay. I wrote stories about gay people and Anne painted their portraits. Our cats were even named Jane and Helen.

As I slipped into my Birkenstocks, I realized she had island fever. She meant Gay Glitz.

"I saw an ad for a lesbian cabaret in Vancouver the weekend of your birthday," I said, pouring the coffee. "Do you want to go?"

"Sure."

. . .

A few weeks later, we stood shivering in a line outside of Uncle Charlie's lounge.

"I'm glad you gave me this," Anne said, snuggling into her new parka.

She looked smashing. The raspberry colored parka set off her wavy gray hair, pink cheeks, and blue eyes. I was proud to be seen with my trim, well-dressed, 48-year-old love.

Soon quite a crowd of young women gathered.

"Susan, why are all these women wearing leather?" Anne asked.

Just then the doors opened and we were swept in. "We" being 198 leather-clad, handcuff-jingling dykes, and my raspberry sweetie and me, the original built-for-comfort, middle aged softie.

The doorwoman cum bouncer eyed us questioningly.

We found seats and began serious woman watching. Talk about well-built bodies!

I whispered to Anne, "Don't do anything provocative, dear, I'd hate to have to defend your honor in this crowd."

A particularly attractive woman with small leather straps running over her bare shoulders and crisscrossing between her naked breasts, one of which had a safety pin through the nipple, squeezed past us to join friends a few seats along. Astonishment on her face Anne asked, "What did you say the name of this show was anyway?"

"Butches in Leather: Bitches in Heat."

"You mean you brought me to a ...." Her indignation turned to curiosity. "Is this what they call exploring your sexuality?"

"Could be fun," I replied, nodding toward the cigarette girl. We savored this long stemmed rose who could have passed for Greta Garbo's great granddaughter. Such shapely legs and so sexy in those black nylons with the seams up the back. They disappeared teasingly into panties barely covered by a fringe skirt. Ohhh....

Then the show began, that is, the show on stage. The other one had started on the sidewalk outside. Both were great fun.

The MC, a striking blonde, appeared dressed as a traditional bride. A bit tarnished, mind you, but still a bride. Her spicy wit alone was worth the price of admission.

The first skit featured the toughest bulldyke Dracula ever to stride across the earth. At the skit's climax she bit the jugular of this sweet young thing. As blood ran down sweetie's peaches and cream chest, I wondered if it were Heinz or just No Name.

The next skit told the story of young Innocent's first visit to a piercing parlor. Polly, the parlor's proprietor, extolled the joys of the pierced life to Innocent and handed her a pictorial catalogue.

"Take your time and don't worry about money. I have a

special pierce and pay by plastic plan. Be back in a sec, hun."

Innocent, who would soon have to change her name, leafed through the pages. Her eyes grew wider and her gasps louder with each page.

Polly returned. "Any questions?' she asked.

"What's a clit?" was Innocent's first question followed by "Will a nipple ring wear a hole in my bra?" Polly explained it all.

Innocent turned the page. A confused look appeared on her face. "Labia major?" she mused. "I think that's what my uncle was in Vietnam. Or was it lieutenant major?"

My favorite skit was the tantalizing striptease by a lithe lovely. As she removed layer after layer of metal and leather, my eyes bulged, my throat became parched, and my temperature rose. At last she wore only black boots with spurs and jangly chains. By this time my eyes were resting on my cheeks and my throat and temperature were positively Saharan. Waves of hormones surged through my body.

I pictured myself ravishing this booted beauty. I could feel her lips yield to my demanding mouth as I ran my hands expertly over her shoulders and onto her voluptuous breasts. She threw back her head moaning with desire. In my mind's eye I saw myself drop to my knees in front of her and bury my face in her luxuriant bush. She trembled as I caressed the backs of her legs, first her delectable thighs, then the tender hollows behind her knees, and finally her curvaceous calves. My fingers slid over the tops of her boots and onto the spurs. My libido withered without a whimper at the thought of being caught in a passionate, thrusting leg-lock with those spurs pressed against my fourth lumbar. That's the one between my compressed discs that "goes out" every so often.

The real life booted tease left the stage amidst thunderous clapping, stomping, and cheering. The earthy blonde MC appeared, dragging her soiled bridal train behind her. "We'll have a 20 minute intermission," she announced. "And remember all you lusty wimmin, no fightin', fuckin', snortin' or smokin' up. At least inside!" Raucous laughter filled the room.

As I turned to Anne to ask if she wanted a drink of mineral water, I saw her glance at her watch and stifle a yawn. "Do you want to go?" I asked, feeling a tad tired myself after my imaginary romp. "Well, it is almost midnight," she said. "And you know what happened to Cinderella." Cinderella? I found it distinctly difficult to associate a glass slipper and Prince Charming with the present crowd of muscled, metalled dykes on their way to either the bar or outside.

Later in bed I cuddled against Anne and fell asleep instantly. I don't recall having any dreams, but I do remember a restless period during which I checked my body for rings of any kind. With a sigh of relief at finding only a gold band with a small diamond on one of my fingers, I drifted into slumber again.

Upon waking in the morning I feasted on the image of the booted beauty that floated seductively in my mind. Ohhhh, I could smell her. I could taste her. I could hear the jingle of her spurs. Then I felt a twinge of pain in my lower back. I ran my hand over it. No blood – darn it! Must be those damned discs.

MORE TO COME

Pamela Pratt

I paused on my way across the office and let my hand sprawl casually on her desk. She looked it over carefully before glancing up to see to whom it belonged. She wasn't quick and nervous, like the other secretaries. "Hi," I said, "I'm Liz Enright. I work in Legal. I haven't seen you here before, you must be new."

"I'm Best Brown. I just started here this week."

"As in *The* best?"

"It's a nickname. That all right with you?"

"I don't dare ask where you got it."

"Try me."

"I might just take you up on that."

She looked me over appraisingly. She wasn't friendly or unfriendly, just biding her time. She had a backwoods drawl, a bad haircut, and I just knew that her desk concealed a pair of sensible shoes.

The company had a dress code, but it should have made an exception in her case. Her suit was cheap and fitted badly. Her broad shoulders looked as though they would rip the jacket apart if she so much as breathed. She did not belong in a skirt and clearly didn't want to be in one. I just knew her knees were spread far apart in an unladylike pose behind the modesty panel of her desk.

I had been passing through the typing pool on my way to deliver some papers to my boss' boss when I saw her. It wasn't any one thing that made me speak to her, and I wasn't known as Miss Congeniality at the office, either. Rather, it was a multitude of small inconsistencies that add up to a particular thing when you know what you're looking for, or what you're looking at.

"What brought you here?" I asked, flicking the edges of some papers on her desk with my fingernails.

"No offense, honey, but why do people usually work?"

"They want to eat, I suppose. They want to pay rent. I meant *here*, why here, not why. You work for love, perhaps. How do *I* know," I said.

"Maybe that's why *you* work, babe," Best said dryly.

I didn't want to lose this round: I changed the subject. "Have you lived in New York long?"

"I just moved here from Maine," Best said, before she remembered to be guarded.

"You lived on a farm?" I asked. She stiffened a little, but it was hard to tell. "Your muscles," I said. "Your back, your shoulders. You're so firm." She nodded, softening. "Whatever made you leave?"

"My friend and I...it didn't work out," she finished, shrugging her shoulders at me.

"C'est la vie," I said.

"Que sera sera," she returned.

So, square one of her life had been colored in for me, at least: in the shape of a pink triangle – as if I'd needed verification. My thigh had found its way onto her desk, and I was rubbing the silk of my dress up and down, slowly, with my Fire Engine Red fingernails. The dress was lavender, and my rings that day were all gold and amethyst to match. Best stopped watching my face. She did my hand justice, taking it in on its trip up and down my thigh as though she were watching a never before performed high wire act.

I stood up and smoothed down the creases in my dress very slowly. I had what I wanted. "Maybe I'll see you around sometime," I said. I didn't need a great exit line when I had Best's eyes glued to my body as I walked away and let the doors of her office swing shut behind me.

The way she had looked at me, like I was candy, I was used to. But I knew she wouldn't come after me – not quite yet, anyhow. There was something made her wary: she couldn't decide if I was the enemy or not – part of the system that would keep a woman like her in the chains of a cheap skirt, or whether I was just an unpoliticized victim. I also knew it wouldn't take much to draw her out. Normally I would have dragged it out a little longer, but I was bored. I stopped by her desk once the next week, and then found myself in her office everyday of the week after that. On a Friday she asked me to have a drink with her. "But you'll have to choose where, I haven't been in town long enough to know where to go yet." She still wasn't sure – or she was sure but not taking any chances.

"The Angel is good, on Sheridan Square," I said. A lesbian bar.

"Shall we go right from work?" she asked.

"Why don't we meet there at six o clock," I suggested.

"That's silly, we get off at the same time, let's walk over there together." She truly didn't understand.

"Please take this in the spirit in which it is intended," I said, "but I would prefer not to be seen leaving with you."

"What about the way you talk to me all the time?" she asked. "If you're worried about your reputation."

"I'm about to make up for that by rubbing my boss' back, and then he'll tell the boys in the washroom and everyone will think I'm having an affair with him. If they have too much to talk about, they won't know what is true."

On my way out of the typing pool I stopped to chat with a male secretary, hopping up onto his desk and resting one of my heels on the edge of his chair. I was wearing a black raw silk skirt with a slit up the side and I flexed my leg up and down, willing Best to watch.

As it happened, she and I ran into each other on the street a block from the bar. She had changed her clothes before she left work and was wearing what she should have been wearing all along: jeans, heavy key ring, work shirt, and a red bandanna around her neck. I changed my mind about where I wanted to go, and we went to a straight place where I was friends with the bartender. We ate peanuts and I drank martinis while Best tried to quiz me about my life. "It's not important," I said. "I think you know everything you need to know."

She was a little taller than me: even with me in my heels she could look straight down into my eyes. "Do you do this a lot?" she asked – but not as though the answer would make a difference.

I shook my hair back and ran my fingers down through it. I tossed off the rest of the martini. I sucked and nibbled on the olive, while staring intently into her eyes. She was so adept that I didn't realize she was undoing the buttons of my skirt until her fingers touched me. There was only pantyhose between us. She left the top button of the skirt done, so it wouldn't slide to the floor. It was a crowded bar, but very dark, and we were in a corner. There was the beginning of a run in my pantyhose at the crotch and Best forced her fingers through it. I gripped the edge of the bar as she moved her hand about, flicking two fingers in and out of me and smearing my wetness down my thighs.

"Don't say a word," she whispered. She put one arm protectively around my waist so that we would appear to be in a close embrace, nothing more. My ankles wobbled. Saliva drooled onto my lip. Her fingers flew back and forth and then were gone. Outside my pantyhose again, she squeezed me once and did up the buttons of my skirt. "You can't just stop," I said. *"Please."*

"I know you want to get fucked real bad, Honey, but a bar is no place to do it in."

"Where can we go?" I whimpered.

"I thought you lived around here."

"I do. I...have a roommate."

She cast me a look. "It's like that, huh? Oh, Christ. Well, I'm not fucking you in no bar."

"I thought that's what you *were* doing."

"That," she said. "That was just an appetizer. I will kiss you, though. I like kissing girls in straight places." Her kiss was surprisingly soft but I drew back from it because of the kind of bar we were in.

"Not here," I murmured.

"More rules? I don't play by rules." She took the fingers that had been inside me and passed them beneath my nose. She slid one finger at a time in and out of my mouth and down my chin. "Oh, I bet your tits are sweet," she sighed. "If I ever get to see them."

I forgot about my rules, too. "Let's get out of here."

"Where to?"

"Don't you have a place, Best?"

"It's all the way uptown."

"Okay, let's do it."

"Wait a minute." She looked apologetic. "I can't. I uh, I have a date at nine o'clock."

"You what?"

"I said I have a date, okay?"

"What was *this*? Do you stack them up?"

"What was this? How in hell was I supposed to know what this was. This pretty bitch at work comes on to me like all get out, and she's straight as hell from what I hear, but how she looks *at* me is something else. So I figure I want to check it out. Do I figure I'm going to be fucking this babe in a bar an hour later? No, I do not. So, I got myself a date at nine o'clock."

I threw money on the bar and walked out. The way I was feeling I would be at the Angel picking someone up in five minutes, to finish off what Best had started. She caught up with me down the block. "Hey. You've no call to be getting so mad."

I pouted a little, then gave in. "I'm not angry," I admitted, "I'm fucking horny." We were walking slower now, down Gay Street, toward the Northern Dispensary, where Waverly Place crosses Waverly Place. "Pretty neat, huh?" I pointed the street sign out to her.

Farther down the block she pulled me suddenly into a doorway. She didn't bother with the buttons this time, just pulled my skirt up, and ripped the crotch out of my pantyhose so that her whole hand could get at me. She bit into my neck, hard. "Hey, no scars, okay?" My hands fluttered in the air in minimal protest.

"Frig your rules," she said savagely, but substituted lips for teeth. I could feel her tongue in the cords of my neck, and down my throat. The tip of her tongue flickered back and forth as fast and as precisely as her fingers did in my cunt; a third finger just whispered its way past my clit. My breasts felt so heavy I thought they would burst from my bra; my knees were shaking. I kicked off my high heels and wedged my back against the door for support. I was moaning something, but I never know afterwards what it is I have said.

"Let me fuck you, baby," she said. "In the fucking street I'm fucking you, come for me, baby, come for me," and she punctuated her murmurings with firmer thrusts into my cunt, or teeth where her tongue had been on my neck a second before.

I don't take long. I rarely have time for long. The first time I came she had to clamp her hand down on my mouth and I realized dimly that she was looking around over her shoulder to see if anyone had noticed. I couldn't stop: she kept bringing me along by touching me less and less. The last time, when I was too sore for much, the heat her wet hand gave off when placed just lightly against my clit was all it took. Then I couldn't stand anything more, even though there was lots of longing left in me.

She turned around and stood guard while I rearranged my clothes and made myself respectable. "I'll walk you to the subway," I said primly, when I was all put back together.

"Isn't that my role?" she laughed. "To make sure you get home safely.."

"You got me off, don't worry about it.."

She looked at me strangely. We knew nothing about each other except heat. "Tomorrow's Saturday," she said. I waited. I can be cruel. And I hate making plans. "Do you want to come over?" she asked finally.

"Why don't I call you when I get up?" I said. "I may have lots of errands to do.."

"I won't call you," she said, as she descended the subway stairs.

"You can't – my number's unlisted," I called down to her, but I doubted that she heard me. I wondered if she'd wait around for my call. I wondered if she'd fret about it till she saw me at work on Monday. I wondered if she'd smell her fingers and dream of me, or if her nine o'clock date would smell me on her first.

I wondered if I'd give in and call her. I wanted more – but then, I always do. I was on my way home to my lover, to tell her all about it, and let her use up all the longing I had left inside.

♀

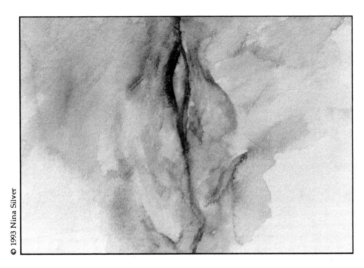

© 1993 Nina Silver

BIRTHING YONI

CONTRIBUTORS
Other Than the Editor, Pamela Pratt

Carrot Juice/Top of the Morning
Donna Allegra

Donna writes fiction, poetry, essays and cultural journalism. Her work has been published in issues of *Sinister Wisdom, Common Lives/Lesbian Lives, Conditions and Heresies.* She has been anthologized in *The Original Coming Out Stories* edited by Julia Penelope and Susan J. Wolfe; *Lesbian Love Stories, Vol. II,* edited by Irene Zahava; *The Persistent Desire,* a femme-butch reader edited by Joan Nestle; *Lesbian Poetry,* edited by Elly Bulkin and Joan Larkin; *Home Girls – A Black Feminist Anthology; Sister/Stranger: Lesbians Loving Across the Lines,* edited by Jan Hardy; and *Quickies: Lesbian Short Shorts,* edited by Irene Zahava. She is the 1992 co-winner of the Pat Parker Memorial Poetry Prize sponsored by *Woman in the Moon Publications.* Her reviews have appeared in *Womanews, Gay Community News, Sojourner, Sappho's Isle* and over WBAI radio where she was formerly a producer and engineer. She works as a construction electrician and is a dancer in African folklore and jazz.

Redheads
Sally Bellerose

Sally writes fiction and poetry. Her work has appeared in numerous journals and anthologies, most recently, *Women on Women 2, Sister/Stranger, A Loving Voice, The Persistent Desire, Women's Glibber,* and *The Poetry of Sex.* The story in this collection was previously published by Alyson Ivers.

⟨♀⟩

Care in the Holding
Maureen Brady

Maureen is author of the novels *Give Me Your Good Ear* and *Folly*, the ahort stories *The Question She Put To Herself*, and the non-fiction books, *Daybreak* and *Beyond Survival: A Writing Journey for Healing Childhood Sexual Abuse* (Harper San Francisco). She has received grants from The Ludwig Vogelstein Foundation, The Barbara Deming Memorial Fund, CAPS, and the New York State Council on the Arts writer in residence program. She teaches writing workshops, sometimes practices Physical Therapy, and divides her time between New York City and the Catskills. Her novel, *Folly*, will be reprinted by The Feminist Press in Spring, 1994. This story was originally published in Feminary, and also in her collection of short stories, *The Question She Put To Herself*.

The Ballad of Mother Fargo
X. P. Callahan

X.P. has published essays, literary criticism, and translations of French, Spanish and Latin American poetry and fiction, most recently in *Calyx* and *The Taos Review*. In 1991, she was awarded a Barbara Deming Memorial Fund grant for her translations of poems by the Argentinian writer, Graciela Reyes, and those translations were published by the Argentinian Consulate in Chicago in 1992. Her work in progress includes a collection of polyphonic prose texts called *Transports*, as well as an English translation of Luis Cernuda's *Ocnos*. The story included in this collection is taken from her own collection in progress to be titled *Grief and Other Stories*. The author lives in Seattle.

Beyond Submission
Sharon Carroll

Sharon lives in Brooklyn, New York, and divides her time among writing, graphic design, cycling, and the W.O.W. (Women's One World) theater collective in Manhattan. She has published fiction, poetry, and arts criticism.

In Front of Everybody
Deborah Kay Ferrell

The author lives in Tallahassee, Florida.

Among the Creatures of Habit
Dianna Hunter

This story is Dianna Hunter's first published work of fiction. She is a northern Minnesota writer, and a former farmer. Her writing has appeared in *Hurricane Alice, A View From the Loft*, and *National Parks Magazine*. Her book, *Breaking Hard Ground*, was published by *Holy Cow! Press* of Duluth. She is currently a middle-aged graduate student at Iowa State University.

The Ad
Tori Joseph

Tori Joseph is a 37 year old writer of lesbian erotica and satire. Her works have appeared in *Deneuve* and *Bad Attitude*. She lives on Cape Cod with her faithful companion, Remy.

Flashback
Karen Latimer

Flashback is a chapter from *Saving The World for a Hobby*, Karen's novel in progress, about the love between a lesbian multimedia artist and a woman politician. The author has had poems and essays published in literary journals, and she is the author of the poetry chapbooks *Intersection, Home of Beautiful Feathers*, and *Love's Country*. She is working on a book of essays, *Neon Buddhic Overdrive: Politics, Sex, and Spirituality – An American Collage*. She lives in New York City, dreaming of trees and flowered acres.

Of My Own Accord
Pam McArthur

The author is a lesbian writer living in the Boston area. Her work has appeared in *Common Lives/Lesbian Lives, Bay Windows,* the magazine, *Backspace,* and the best-selling anthology, *Bushfire.*

My Raspberry Sweetie and Me
Susan McIver

Susan McIver lives with her partner, Anne, on Salt Spring Island, British Columbia, and writes humorous stories.

Shoes
Claire Olivia Moed

The author is a native New Yorker, playwright and performer. She is the author of *How to Say Kaddish With Your Mouth Shut: One Comic Family's Misery, Suicide and Other Lovers, Love Slapped Me Boom, Boom Upside My Head,* and a book/performance piece (and birthday present) to J. L. Wong, *Driven By Passion, Run Over By Love.*

Say My Name
Karen Moulding

The author is an attorney and a graduate student in the Master's Program in Creative Writing at City College of New York, where she teaches English Composition and Humanities. Karen is a graduate of the University of Montana (where she studied writing with William Kittredge and Naomi Lazard), and Columbia University Law School. She writes poetry and fiction, and is currently at work on her second novel, *Fading Under Ivy.* Chair of the Lesbian-Gay Committee of the National Lawyers Guild, Karen is Editor of the Sixth Edition of the treatise "Sexual Orientation and the Law."

Monday Night at the Movies
Lesléa Newman

Author of 12 books and the editor of two anthologies, Lesléa's latest works are: a novel, *In Every Laugh A Tear*; a poetry collection, *Sweet Dark Places*; and an anthology, *Eating Our Hearts Out: Women and Food*. She has recently completed a short story collection, *Every Woman's Dream*. Since writing the story in this collection, she has not been discovered at the corner of Hollywood and Vine or elsewhere.

Prologue
Sarah Schulman

Sarah is the author of five novels, *Empathy* (Dutton, 1992), *People In Trouble* (Dutton, 1990), winner of the Gregory Koloukos Memorial Prize for AIDS writing, *After Delores* (Dutton, 1988), winner of the American Library Asociation Lesbian//Gay Book Award, *Girls, Visions & Everything* (Seal Press, 1986) and *The Sophie Horowitz Story* (NAIAD Press, 1984). Her first non-fiction book, *That Perilous Night: Lesbian and Gay Life During the Reagan/Bush Years, Collected Writings 1981-1992*, will be published in 1994 by Routledge.

Woman in the Window/I Kissed Her on the Street
Patricia Roth Schwartz

Author of the Lambda-award-winning short story collection, *The Names of the Moons of Mars*, Schwartz has published fiction in *Bushfire: Stories of Lesbian Desire*, *Lesbian Love Stories II*, *Unholy Alliances*, *Afterglow: More stories of Lesbian Desire*, and her poetry has appeared in *Wanting Women*. Besides writing, she teaches at the college level, practices psychotherapy privately, and owns Weeping Willow Farm, where she raises herbs, organic produce, and Christmas trees. Her family consists of cats, dogs, and rabbits.

The Maturing of Mooghan
Nina Silver

Nina Silver is a Reichian therapist whose writing on feminism, sexuality, the natural sciences, and metaphysics has appeared in *The New Internationalist, off our backs, Empathy, Gnosis, Green Egg, Jewish Currents, Common Lives/Lesbian Lives,* and the anthologies *Women's Glib, Lesbian Bedtime Stories, Childless By Choice, Wanting Women, Closer to Home: Bisexuality and Feminism, Cats (and their Dykes), Eating Our Hearts Out, Transforming a Rape Culture, and VeriTales.* Her volume of poetry, *Birthing*, will be published in 1994 by Woman in the Moon Publications. She has just completed a book integrating feminism, depth psychology, and the body/mind principles of Wilhelm Reich.

Breakfast/Carrying Coals to Newcastle
Cody Yeager

A Ph.D. candidate at the University of Oregon, the author's work has appeared in *Timberline, Womyn's Press, West Wind Review* and others. She lives with her two dogs and sometimes talks to the possum who lives under her house; sometimes he talks back.

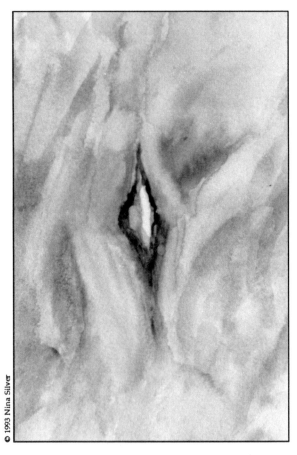

PROUD YONI

THE ARTWORK

Nina Silver's love of beauty and color, together with her love of women, have inspired her twelve watercolors of Yoni, nine of which are reproduced in this book in black and white. Several of the watercolors were originally hung at The Gallery in Newport, Rhode Island, for a 1992 exhibit of women's sacred art. She says, "Painting for me has been a relaxing and intensely meditative experience. More importantly, though, I have learned that for women, affirmatively naming and honoring our sexual organ – which is part of celebrating our wholeness – is deeply healing." Nina is currently negotiating for her watercolor Yoni to be available for wider distribution, on notecards and possibly a calendar. For more information, she can be reached c/o Healing Heart Music, P.O. Box 293, New York, NY 10025, USA.

ABOUT THE EDITOR

The editor of this book, Pamela Pratt, died on March 28, 1993, from diabetes-related causes. She was 35 years old.

Pamela was the director of the "In Our Own Write" reading and writing workshop. She was published often in literary journals and her stories appear in *Lesbian Love Stories, Vol. II* and *Word of Mouth, Vol. II.* She resided in New York City. She is survived by her parents.

STARbooks Press thanks Pamela's parents and all of the contributors to this book for being a part of what has become a fitting tribute to a wonderful woman and gifted writer.

Pamela Pratt
1958-1993

A TRIBUTE

Donna Allegra

I met Pamela VerVeer Pratt in Paula Martinac's class, *Writing Lesbian Lives*, in the fall of 1990. I was immediately attracted to such a good writer so, after the first session, I followed her on my bike so that we could talk. After the course was over, some of us continued to meet at Pamela's Soho apartment, and when the group faded, she and I remained friends.

We became writing partners. I loved and respected her work, which has appeared in issues of *Sinister Wisdom*, *On Our Backs*, *Visibilities*, *Lesbian Love Stories, Vol. II*, edited by Irene Zahava; *What's a Nice Girl Like You Doing in a Relationship Like This?* published by *Crossing Press*, *Word Of Mouth, Vol. II*, edited by Irene Zahava; and *Sideshow*, an anthology of contemporary American Writings, published by *Somersault Press* in 1991. We'd meet in various cafes to write and share current projects. She'd have her ever-present espresso and infernal cigarettes, and I'd have herbal tea with a tolerance for passive smoke. She frequently checked her blood-sugar level with paraphernalia I found fascinating. She had childhood-onset diabetes and was insulin-dependent.

In 1991, she became chair of the Lesbian and Gay Community Center's *In Our Own Write* literary reading series. She was dedicated to the project and put in innumerable hours, delighting in the work. She wrote individual letters to all her readers. I told her this was madness, but that's what she did.

She also founded the Writers Workshops at the Lesbian and Gay Community Center. She cared about writers and writing, read voraciously, and once said her ideal job would be to own a bookstore. We talked books, traded calls for submission. I valued that friendship and don't know that I'll have such a literary buddy again. I looked forward to our respective novel work - it would be her second novel. I knew her book would interest me and that her feedback would make me a better writer.

The Friday before she died, she told me she'd had a scare about losing her eye sight due to nerve damage from the diabetes. The doctor had told her that day that it looked like the problem cleared up and she was no longer in danger of going blind. She was so elated that she went out and spent $150.00 on books at the Oscar Wilde Memorial Bookstore.

I was also angry at her, watching her declining health over the past year. She was ill and I didn't know how to make her take better care of herself. She still smoked incessantly and drank espresso, which only exacerbated her diabetes. Lecturing that stubborn lady would have been counter-productive. She'd had pneumonia and other crises of health during the last months. She spoke of insomnia. She sometimes had to check her blood as many as 15 times a day. Doctors say that when diabetics get to this stage, their lives become intolerable.

I didn't know what it meant to live with chronic illness. I don't know if she knew my anger came from caring. I wish now I'd been more compassionate and openly loving in my concern. Every way I turn, I grieve the loss. A wonderful woman gone too soon, too young.

ANOTHER TRIBUTE

Patricia Roth Schwartz

Two days after Pamela died, I received in my mailbox a huge package of some of her favorite books she was lending me – *Housekeeping* by Marilynne Robinson, *Annie John* by Jamaica Kinkaid, the new Sandra Scoppetone lesbian mystery to which she'd treated herself in hardcover – as well as a cheery card. At first glance I recoiled, then quickly welcomed the package as I now treasure the books as a way to hang on a little longer to my dear friend.

Pamela Pratt, to our communities, was the tireless organizer of the "In Our Own Write" Reading Series. She called me to invite me to be in the series because she'd read my book and and loved it. I agreed to attend and she put me up at her apartment.

She was also the writer of exquisite stories of rare grace and high literary style. She was the considerate and imaginative editor of this anthology.

To me, she was the one I could call at 11:00 p.m. anytime and tell her anything. Her wisdom was amazing. Her support was one of my blessings in a bleak time.

She was the one who showed up to spend five days with me over what would have been a tough Thanksgiving, so I wouldn't have to spend it alone. Then she spent much of those days helping me work on my much-in-process house.

She was the one who relentlessly encouraged my writing even when life events made me feel I couldn't keep at it.

She was the one who offered to do writers' workshops with me over the phone and by mail. We never got to do that. I'll have to carry on now without her. My next book will likely be dedicated to her.

I'll be seeing her perky little face and her slender, black leather-clad body forever and hear her welcoming and raspy voice greeting me over the phone at 11:00 p.m.

The work she did for us all and the words she wrote remain with us, her legacy.